OBSESSIONS

.

CYBERWEBS III

OBSESSIONS

■

CYBERWEBS III

MIRANDA REIGNS

BLUE MOON BOOKS
NEW YORK

Published by
Blue Moon Books
An Imprint of Avalon Publishing Group Incorporated
841 Broadway, Fourth Floor
New York, NY 10003

OBSESSIONS: CYBERWEBS III

ISBN 1-56201-234-7

Printed in the United States of America

Distributed by Publishers Group West

This novel is dedicated to "Miranda"...
The hidden voice inside us all...
That has the right to remain silent...
Or not.

This novel is also dedicated to my friend
Simon Caan
Who inspired my inner poet
Through his erotic expressions
By means of Haiku.

CHAPTER 1

∎

CONFESSIONS

Obsessed. That's the only way to describe it. Russ is completely and utterly obsessed, the desire to have his way with me consuming every waking moment. It wasn't always like this. Russ used to be a good friend, well, of my husband, happy go lucky, yet always with a perverted twist. Never were his sexual advances directed at or towards me, not until the poker game, that is. Ever since that poker game . . . ever since he *lost* that poker game, things have been different.

It wasn't your usual game of poker by far, but a rather unorthodox one with yours truly as the grand prize. Although it was exciting at the time, it is an experience I'd rather not repeat. The winner of each hand was allowed only a minute to use and fondle my body at will, the only stipulations being no penile penetration and nothing that was harmful or dangerous. Although Russ did manage to win a couple of hands, he was not the big winner of the night.

* * *

Jerome . . . big, black, beautiful Jerome came out on top and was offered my services for an entire hour. This time, fucking was allowed, and Jerome took me every which way imaginable, a sight which proved to be more than Russ could handle. He left that night very disgruntled and agitated, and let Nick and I know on a daily basis how wronged he felt. After all, Nick and I have a very open marriage, and if I am allowed extra-marital affairs, why couldn't he be one of the recipients?

Now, six months later, I am still receiving bizarre e-mails from Russ, only this one a little more threatening, a little more menacing. Unable to keep the shivers from climbing up my spine, I read his chilling words once again . . .

Miranda . . . I keep remembering how your body swallowed up Jerome's cock, and how I wished it were mine instead, ramming mercilessly into you. Oh, and that ass . . . that sweet, fuckable ass was meant to be mine. I shall have it someday.

I've been watching you dress . . .

The arms you caress . . .

As you try to decide what to wear.

I've been watching the way . . .

You get ready each day . . .

The results are most charming, my dear.

A blouse made of silk . . .

Covers shoulders of milk . . .

But can never disguise what's beneath.

And panties of floral . . .

Can't hide what's immoral . . .

A hot wanton womanly sheath.

And you stroke oh so tender . . .
Long legs, smooth and slender . . .
Each time that you put on your hose.
And with earnest precision . . .
Your skirt has arisen . . .
Revealing a dew-moistened rose.

Slowing turning around . . .
To reach for the ground . . .
Rewards me with one tiny peek.
A glimpse of a thigh . . .
As it stretches . . . my, my . . .
And the bottom of each little cheek.

You are heaven in motion . . .
Causing quite the commotion . . .
To not touch you is physical pain.
The sensuous way . . .
I watch your hips sway . . .
The pleasure is mine soon to gain.

I've been watching you dress . . .
And my cock I caress . . .
As I dream of the day I shall have you.
All twisted in passion . . .
My own special fashion . . .
In a dungeon I've built to contain you.

When I finish my game . . .
My mark will forever be left upon you.

Dear God . . . the man is insane.

*   *   *

"Nick!"

"What?! What is it Miranda? You sound panicked."

"I am . . . oh, God . . . read this latest e-mail from Russ. I think he's gone over the edge."

"Wow. I didn't know he was a poet!"

"God damn it, Nick! That's not what I'm talking about. I'm truly scared!"

"Sorry, sorry. Just trying to lighten the moment with a little humor, that's all. Want me to have a talk with him? Tell him the game is over and to quit pestering you?"

"Do you think that will work?"

"Yeah . . . Russ isn't dangerous. He's just a pervert. I think he's trying to talk your language to entice you. I believe that he thinks this letter will turn you on. Did it? Maybe just a little?"

"Uh . . . what a fucked up question, Nick. No . . . no . . . Of course not!"

"I don't believe you."

Without warning, Nick grabs the rear of my chair and begins to roll me backwards, away from the computer desk, then swivels me around to face him. Searching my eyes deeply, he asks again, "Are you sure you're not even remotely excited by that letter?"

Nervously I answer, "No. For Pete's sake. I said I wasn't, now let's please just drop it."

A malicious grin slowly spreads from ear to ear across his handsome face.

*　　*　　*

4

"If I find out that you're lying to me, Miranda, I'm going to have to spank you," he warns teasingly.

With his eyes never leaving mine, he crouches down in front of me and places his hand on my bare knee. Slowly, he begins to move his hand upward along the inside of my thigh, causing me to shiver and gasp at his intentions. His hand disappears under my short skirt to moments later confront the evidence I can no longer conceal.

"Tsk, tsk, tsk, Miranda. Your panties are soaked! I'd say Russ's letter did a mite more than you admitted earlier. Now answer me again. Does the thought of being taken into Russ's dungeon excite you?"

My words are cut short as I feel Nick's fingers begin to stroke me, swirling themselves around on my drenched panties, rubbing in circles across the satin barrier. Back and forth his fingers travel, starting up high at my clit and circling down to my opening. Forgetting that I am supposed to reply, I moan and lean back in the chair, closing my eyes, surrendering to the sensations of his expert fingers. Nick continues to masturbate me gently, his thumb now taking over, still taking care to remain above my panties.

"Oh yes, I'd say that it does, my little whore wife."

Shaking my head, I try to deny it, but am unable to speak the words. My hips begin to rock and thrust upwards, begging for something more.

*　　*　　*

"Please, Nick, please . . ."

"Please, what, baby?"

"Please take me there. . . ."

"Not until you're honest with me."

Still, his thumb continues its gentle assault, stealing yet more moisture from my throbbing pussy to become absorbed into the already dripping crotch of my panties. Back and forth, up and down, gentle circles teasing, causing me to buck wildly. With my head thrown back over the top of the chair, my hands assume a death grip on the handles.

Panting now, I beg him for release.

"Please, Nick. I . . . need . . . more."

"What are the words I want to hear, my little whore wife? What are they?"

Breathless . . . "Okay, okay. . . . Yes, ohhhhh, yes, Russ's letter turned me on. I admit it. Now please . . . "

"Not yet, sweetness. What about Russ's letter turned you on?"

"Ohhhh, Nick."

"Come on, now. I want to enter that depraved little mind of yours. Tell me."

Nick's thumb continues its torturous course, never increasing in speed or pressure, just slowly and methodically working to maintain a high state of arousal, yet allowing nothing more. I wrap my feet behind the wheels of the chair to keep my legs from closing, relishing in the feeling of simulated bondage.

"Oh God, Nick. The thought that he watches me dress and undress. The thought that he witnesses my most private moments."

"My little slut enjoys putting on a show, doesn't she? What else?"

Nick's thumb picks up a little speed as a reward for my cooperation.

"Uh . . . oh, yes. . . . Uh, the thought of him taking me against my will."

"Oh yes. The infamous rape fantasy. How do you want it to happen?"

"I don't . . . I don't . . . want it to happen. . . . it's just a fantasy."

Nick applies more pressure as his own excitement begins to build.

"That's a cop-out answer, Miranda. How? Do you want him to rip your clothes from your body, or fuck you with them still on?"

"Yes . . . oh yes . . ."

"Do you want to feel the head of his dick ramming through your panties, pushing them way up inside you, like this?"

"Eeeeeeeeyyyyyy! Yesssss, yessssss!"

Nick's thumb forces the fabric of my panties as far deep into my pussy as it can reach, stretching the delicate elastic to its limit . . . Then he reaches up with his other hand and grabs my hair, pulling my head back even further and holds it immobile. Choking, I gasp at the aggressive turn this encounter has taken, as his thumb begins to relentlessly penetrate and withdraw from my aching hole. My legs and arms remain rigid and solidly affixed to the chair as if indeed, they truly were bound to it.

"What else?" Nick grunts out through clenched teeth, almost angrily.

"Nothing . . . there's nothing else," I manage to wheeze out despite the angle of my out-stretched neck.

"Nothing? Not even curious about this dungeon he mentions?"

"Oh yes . . . yes the dungeon, too. . . ."

"What about the dungeon excites you, Miranda?"

Nick continues to vigorously fuck me with his thumb, while his hold on my hair remains firm. Just as I begin to answer him, his teeth clamp on to my right nipple through the thin fabric of my sheer blouse.

"OWWWWW!" I wail in protest, but his bite stays constant.

"Go on," he mumbles as he begins to chew and feast on his newest target.

"The. . . . b. . . . bondage . . . the. . . . re . . . restraints . . . all of it. The whips. . . . the paddles . . . everything."

With this last admission, Nick begins to masturbate me with a purpose, no longer content to just play with me. His thumb continues to fuck me while his other four fingers manipulate and rub circles over my throbbing clit. The sensations are compounded by his teeth viciously twisting and pulling at my nipple, taking pleasure in my small little yelps of objection. The pain is not enough to take away from my rapidly approaching orgasm, in fact, only serves to heighten it. Suddenly, I am completely and thoroughly consumed by rapturous spasms and paralyzing convulsions.

As I cry out my release, Nick relinquishes his hold on my nipple and stands to passionately fuse his lips with my own. Kissing me through my final shudder, a disheveled Nick finally takes a step back and begins working on his own problem. The front of his boxers are stained with his arousal, while his raging erection pushes angrily outward. Upon release of his rigid member, Nick once again grabs my hair at the back of my head, forcing me to sit up straight and remain at eye level with his engorged penis. Wrapping his hand around the base of his cock, Nick begins to stroke it and pump it up and down, keeping it within inches of my face. I watch as he jacks off at a fast and furious pace, impatient to reach his own climax. I acknowledge the inevitable swelling of his prick only moments before globs of sticky white cum shoot out and splatter across my face, just as his own satisfied grunts fill the room. He finishes by rubbing his still semi-erect cock all over my face until every drop of his cum is absorbed into my skin.

"Oh, God, Nick. What the hell was that about?"

"Fun, wasn't it?" he answers, mischievously. "But I'm not quite through with you yet. I still owe you a spanking for lying to me."

As a feeling of dread washes over me, I try every tactic I can think of to dissuade Nick.

"I'm sorry, Nick. I didn't mean to lie. I didn't know I was aroused until you discovered it."

*   *   *
———
9

Nick raises his eyebrows in amusement, but says nothing.

"Really, Nick. I thought I was just scared. I guess there's a fine line separating the two. I didn't realize . . ."

Still remaining silent, Nick crosses his arms and waits for me to continue.

"Uh . . . now I know . . . now we both know. What's the big deal?"

"You are so delightful when you panic, Miranda, but a lie is a lie. If you didn't know, you should have just said that you didn't know. Now get up out of that chair and follow me over to the couch."

Nick perches himself on the edge of the couch to wait for my less than enthusiastic arrival. Damn, what is the matter with me? I've been spanked by Nick hundreds of times and I've survived them all blissfully intact. What is it about the threat of a spanking that can reduce a grown woman to a trembling pathetic little waif? As if a spanking was the most horrible torture ever devised! Even rationalizing this has no effect as I close the distance between Nick and me, trying one last desperate plea.

"Please?"

"Miranda, the longer you stall, the angrier I'm going to get. Now get over my knees."

Pouting, I lay myself across his knees, my belly firmly supported by his thighs, my head and arms hanging over one side while my legs dangle over the other. Shifting, he readjusts me so that he is able to lift my skirt completely up and over my ass, unhindered. Mortified, I feel the blood and heat surge to my face. Nick takes his time, dallying to prolong my humiliation, making comments about my ass.

"Mmmmm, no wonder Russ is obsessed with your ass, Miranda. It is beautiful . . . intoxicating . . . especially the way it quivers right before a spanking. I think I'll spank you until I'm hard again, and then fuck you between those rosy red cheeks."

"Oh, God, no, Nick. They'll already be so sore. . . ."

Gently slipping my thong panties down and off my ass and legs, Nick wads them up and stuffs them into my surprised mouth.

"You talk too much. These should help keep you quiet."

Outraged, I begin to kick and squirm, my muffled protests falling on deaf ears.

"That's it, baby. Fight me as I spank the hell out of you. Let's make this interesting."

Soon his hand is rising and falling in rapid succession, giving me little to no time to recover from each swat. Within seconds, my ass is on fire, Nick's large hands leaving lasting imprints on my backside. I continue to kick out and squirm, unable to make my hands of any use. This only goads Nick on, fueling his fire.

"Come on baby . . . where's your spunk? Oh, look at that rosy ass. Mmmmm, mmmmmmm. I'm going to enjoy fucking it. What's that? A squeal? Hmmmm . . . does that hurt, my little whore wife, or does it make you wet? Seventeen . . . Eighteen . . . Nineteen . . . Twenty."

As tears begin to flow freely down my face, Nick pauses to check on his progress. Slipping a finger easily inside my well-lubricated pussy, he comments on his findings.

"Ah, yeah . . . that's it, my baby. Nothing like a good spanking to get those juices flowing freely again. As much as you fight it, you want it."

Removing his finger, he resumes the spanking.

"Twenty-one . . . twenty-two. . . ."

By thirty, I am all but bucking on his thighs, his erection now very noticeably poking me in the side. By forty, Nick decides that I've had enough and stops the spanking just long enough to pull me to a standing position. He kicks off his boxers and then orders me to bend over and grab my ankles. Assisting, he helps to speedily fold me in half, pressing my shoulders over and down. Still not fully recovered from the spanking, I continue to sob and moan as I'm forced to, once again, offer my ass.

Nick's fingers waste no time gathering lubricant from my dripping pussy to spread generously on, around and in my tight little ass. I suck in my breath as I feel the head of his dick press cautiously against it, slowly coaxing it open. I have never before been taken anally in this position, and the sensations are all new and quite thrilling. Suddenly, the stinging heat of my ass is forgotten as I lose myself in the splendor of Nick's cock slowly entering my ass. Nick holds tightly to my hips to keep me from toppling over as I will myself to relax and open for him. Slowly he guides his entire length deep inside my ass and holds still for a few moments so that I may grow accustomed to the intruder.

"Mrrrrumph . . . mmmmmrrrrumph"
   "Yeah, baby. I know."

Nick waits to continue until he is quite certain that I am relaxed and ready, spurred on by the persistent wriggling of my hips. Then he begins to withdraw only to drive back deep into my bowels on the next thrust. Nick fucks my ass over and over again, picking up a little more speed, pulling my hips back towards him as he rams his own cock forward. In and out, in and out, back and forth, back and forth. As the frenzy of the pace increases, so do the groans being torn from Nick's throat.

"Ahhhhh, yeaaaaaah, baby, I'm gonna cum. I'm gonna cuuuuuuuuuummmmmmmmmm.
AHHHHHHHHHHHHHHH!!!!!"

With one final thrust, Nick buries his dick to the hilt and explodes deep in my ass, losing himself in ecstasy. Still gripping my ankles, I wait for him to recover and extract his slackening penis, which slips easily from my well-used anus. Breathing a sigh of relief, I am happy to discover that I have survived yet another one of Nick's terrifying spankings.

Once the sexual tension of Russ's e-mail finally dissipates, Nick and I are able to resume some sense of normality. I return to the computer to finish checking my e-mail, while Nick busies himself with his own little chores. Keeping the conversation light, Nick asks, "Hey, who was the other e-mail from? I noticed you had two of them."

"I'm not sure yet. I'm just now reading it."

Meet me in the chat rooms tonight.

SeaNymph

"Well, I'll be! I think it's from Angela! She must have finally gotten her own computer. She wants me to join her tonight in the chat rooms."

"Angela, the hot redhead? The exotic dancer?"

"Yes, and one of my best friends. Gosh, I haven't heard from her since I've been back home. I feel terrible for not keeping in touch with her!"

"Well, if you'd like, I can explain to her how I've kept you *tied up* since you've been home, allowing you little opportunity for correspondence."

"Depending on how mad she is, I just may have to take you up on that. What a selfish, selfish husband you've been, not letting me stay in contact with my friends."

"I don't think selfish is a subject you should be bringing up at all, Miranda," Nick chastises playfully.

"Touché!" I reply, somewhat embarrassed.

Eager to hear what Angela's been up to, I hurriedly enter the chat rooms and search for her nickname. I locate the *SeaNymph* instantly, and invite her into a private chat.

<Aphrodite> | Angela! How are you? I was so happy to
              get your e-mail!

_____

14

<SeaNymph>	Doing great, Randi. I have so much to tell you.
<Aphrodite>	I'm all ears.
<SeaNymph>	Well, as you can guess, I finally bought my own computer. I've become totally enslaved. It's all I do now when I'm not dancing!
<Aphrodite>	Oh, I know how that goes, believe me. Been there, done that. But don't worry. It will pass soon enough.
<SeaNymph>	And do you remember Antonio? Or should I say, Poseidon?
<Aphrodite>	How can I forget? He was your first on-line orgasm, if I remember correctly.
<SeaNymph>	<blushing> You got that right! Anyway, I've been hooking up with him almost daily in the chat rooms. Apparently, he is a big computer guru who spends most of his time down in Mexico. He's filthy rich from inventing some type of highly advanced Virtual Reality suit.
<Aphrodite>	I don't know, Angela. I think "VR" has been around for a while. Are you sure he invented it?
<SeaNymph>	Maybe not the original design, but he's perfected it. His specialty is "Sex in VR."
<Aphrodite>	Oooo, now that's intriguing. I haven't heard much more than being able to see in 360 degrees. Sex, huh?
<SeaNymph>	Oh yeah. And he builds programs to work in conjunction with the suit. He creates the virtual worlds needed for experiencing the virtual sex. He's a freak-

ing genius! And he's all mine!

\<Aphrodite\> | Wow! And of course, Virtual Sex automatically made you think of your good friend, Miranda!

\<SeaNymph\> | But of course, dahhhling . . . don't be ridiculous. Two peas in a pod!

\<Aphrodite\> | I'm flattered. So have you tried it out? How does it work?

\<SeaNymph\> | No, not yet. I'm afraid to. What if I get stuck in the program or something and my brain fries in real life and turns to mush? Antonio wants to meet me for the first time in VR. I'm scared to death. I had to send him all sorts of information about myself, as well as several nude pictures taken from all angles. He now knows everything about me from the circumference of my head to the color of my toe nails!

\<Aphrodite\> | Wow! It sounds spooky. He can totally re-create you now in a computer image. I don't blame you for being hesitant.

\<SeaNymph\> | But I want to meet him and experience VR so badly. It's tearing me up. Even you and I could meet in person in one of his worlds. (Sex optional, of course! \<evil grin\>)

\<Aphrodite\> | It does sound fantastic. Promise me this, though. If you decide to do it, don't do it alone. Invite Robert or one of the other dancers over and give them explicit instructions on when to interfere. Set a certain time limit, and if you

---

haven't come out on your own by that time, have whomever shut down the computer. Once the computer is off, I'm sure you'll be able to come out of it instantly. Just as a precaution. I'm sure you won't have to resort to that. Just inform Antonio of your time restrictions in advance.

<SeaNymph> | That sounds plausible. Oooo, I knew you'd understand! Hey, can I e-mail you one of Antonio's VR questionnaires? You know, just in case you ever want to join in the fun? It's quite extensive and will most likely take you weeks to complete.

<Aphrodite> | Sure, but I doubt that I'll be able to afford to buy one of the suits. As technical as it all sounds, it probably costs a fortune.

<SeaNymph> | Well, right now we can get in for free, because he is still in his testing phase. He needs guinea pigs to help discover any glitches. Once it is out there for the general public, you can bet it's going to cost a pretty penny. He's assured me over and over that it is completely safe. He just needs confirmation that the experiences and sensations felt in VR closely resemble those of the real world.

<Aphrodite> | Well, if we are ever going to do it, it might as well be now while we can afford it. Go ahead and send me that application or whatever it is.

<SeaNymph> | Ok, it'll be in your e-mail box by tomor-

	row. I have to go now and explain things to Antonio. Oh, Randi, I'm so excited.
<Aphrodite>	Well, I'm not going to get in a tizzy until I'm dressed in the suit and ready to press the "start program" button!
<SeaNymph>	Ta ta. . . . I'll keep in touch with details! Until we re-unite in VR!
<Aphrodite>	Ta ta. . . . See you in VR!!!

What a nut. As much as I'd like to think that Virtual Reality Sex is a possibility, I'm far too skeptical to believe that it truly can work properly. Too many variables exist that are too complicated to recreate. I'll fill out Angela's questionnaire, but with minimal expectations. At the very least, it was great to hear from her again.

Just as I'm about to click out of the chat rooms, another name invites me into a private chat.

<DarkShadows>	Beware of where he lurks . . . Cause despite his many quirks . . . He is hell bent to possess you.
<Aphrodite>	Excuse me?
<DarkShadows>	Be careful where you strut . . . For you see my little slut . . . He knows you as so few do.
<Aphrodite>	Who is this?
<DarkShadows>	Be careful where you roam . . . Don't you wander far from home . . . He might get you if you do so.
<Aphrodite>	Russ? Is that you? Come on, this isn't funny.

<DarkShadows>	Every night and every day . . .
	You'll be forced to play my way . . .
	Putting on a pretty show.
<Aphrodite>	Russ. It doesn't have to be like this.
	Let's talk, please.
<DarkShadows>	Beware of where he sits . . .
	For you know he never quits . . .
	Not until he's won the grand prize.
<Aphrodite>	Come on, now, you're scaring me.
	We're friends, remember?
<DarkShadows>	Beware my little lass . . .
	Soon I'm gonna fuck your ass . . .
	To surrender would be so wise.
<Aphrodite>	I surrender! I surrender! What do you
	need for me to do?

Chat ended.

Damn, damn, damn! Do I tell Nick about this, or will it turn into another spanking session? Wrought with fear and uncertainty, I snuggle up extra close to Nick after climbing into bed, surrounding myself in the safety and protection of his loving arms.

■

CHAPTER 2

DECEPTIONS

A man left incomplete . . .
May wander down the street . . .
Devising evil plans.
A man left on the brink . . .
Has lots of time to think . . .
How he'll use you in his hands.

"Nick! Russ is still at it! I just got another threatening poem from him. I want you to talk to him."

"Ok . . . I'll talk to him. Let me know if you get any more of them."

"You'll be the *first* to know . . ."

Well, at least he waited a week before e-mailing this one to me. For a while there, I was getting them almost daily. He must have just gotten back from a vacation too remote even for his laptop. It's also been almost a month since I returned Antonio's VR questionnaire back to Angela, and am waiting with bated breath for the arrival of my suit. She assured me in her last e-mail that it would be sent within a couple of weeks. The realization that I may soon be participating in Virtual Reality Sex . . . taking place in a make-believe world . . . is finally beginning to pique my curiosity. I can't wait.

"You know, Miranda, I was thinking."

"Yes, Nick."

"How would you feel about getting a job, even if just part time? I think it would be good to get away from the computer and all those psychotic e-mails for a while. They are beginning to consume your thoughts, and I hate to see you so unnerved all the time. It's just a suggestion."

"You know, that's not a bad idea. I've been thinking about it too, but because of Russ, now I'm *afraid* to leave the house. I feel like he's going to follow me and whisk me away at the first opportunity."

"Miranda, if he really wanted to kidnap you, he knows where to find you. I'm gone most of the time and you are left home alone. Coming here would be the easiest way to snatch you up. I told you, he's not dangerous. He's just messing with your head to get back at you for rejecting his advances."

"You really think so?"

"Yes, I really think so. Otherwise, I'd have had him arrested by now for harassing you."

"Well, if you really think I'm safer out in the workforce . . ."

"I think it will improve your peace of mind immensely, not to mention help your social life. Your computer friends are fine, but some real interaction wouldn't hurt you any, either."

"Have anything in mind?"

"Hmmmm . . . just off the top of my head I can tell you that they are looking for a receptionist for that new office building at the corner of 6th and Main. You could easily walk back and forth to work each day."

"That's sounds perfect. I'll call them."

It feels strange being back in the formal nine to five atmosphere. Although it is just the interview, I feel as if I already have the job. I glance around the reception area, beautifully decorated and spotlessly new, but sorely neglected. The coffee pot is almost empty, with the remaining contents close to burning. Newspapers and magazines are haphazardly scattered about. The plants are drooping, positively dying from thirst, and the phones keep ringing, unanswered. Well, if not me, they'd better hire someone fast before they lose tons of business.

I take it upon myself to begin straightening things out while I wait. A kind man informs me that "the boss" will see me shortly, and that he is still with a previous applicant. He also apologizes for having to immediately abandon me, but he has a quick errand to run. Of course, I am to make myself comfortable in the interim.

First, I quickly organize the magazines and arranged them neatly on the table. Then I toss out all the old newspapers, keeping only the ones from today. Next I wander over to the coffee and sink area and begin to brew a fresh pot. Finally, I find an empty glass and use it to water the poor, overlooked plants. I find myself tempted to answer the phones as well, but struggle to curb that urge. I'm not even sure of the name of the company . . . how can I possibly answer their telephone?

Sitting back down once again, I glance at my outfit. I had chosen a basic black skirt, mid- to upper-thigh length, accented by a pale pink silk blouse. I am also wearing black thigh high stockings and a pair of classic black heels. The outfit isn't anything too fancy, just a nice, professional look. I also chose to wear my hair down, not wanting to give the impression that I was too severe or rigid. Intent on removing a piece of lint from my skirt, I miss his entrance.

"Uh hum . . . excuse me . . . ma'am?"

"Oh, hello. Sorry, I never knew a piece of lint could be so fascinating," I offer humorously.

Smiling, he says, "My name is Wesley. Mr. Miller will see you now."

"Hello, Wesley. I'm Miranda. Pleased to meet you," I respond, as he gallantly shakes my extended hand.

I follow him down several corridors until we stop outside a closed office door.

"Just a word of warning. Mr. Miller is a very nice man, but he's a little out there."

"What do you mean?"

"He doesn't ever let anybody see him. A curtain separates his desk from the rest of his office and he sits behind it while he conducts meetings and interviews. Rumor has it that he suffered a terrible injury that left him physically deformed."

"Oh! The poor man! It must be horrible to have to live your life like that! He should just come out and face it. People would accept him more readily than he thinks."

"Rumor also has it that he is very vain. Nobody has ever seen him, yet he runs his companies flawlessly."

"He has more than one?"

"Yes, several. He spends a couple of years setting them up and making sure they are running properly, then goes off to buy another one." Whispering conspiratorially, "And. . . . they say he travels only at night. . . ."

"Ohhhh . . . if you don't mind my asking, what exactly is the name of this company and what does it do?"

"It's called *Handymans*. Basically, it's a service used mostly by women to hire a man to do things around the house that she herself doesn't feel comfortable doing . . . or just plain doesn't want to do. You know, things like mowing the lawn, putting up shelves in the kid's room, taking the car in for a service, shoveling snow, those sorts of things. Our fees are very reasonable, and already hundreds of calls have come in. We've only been here a month, but it's been long enough to get the word out. Mr. Miller is still trying to hire enough men to fill all of the requests. As you can see, we need a receptionist very badly."

"Sounds like it would be a lot of fun to work here. I can't wait to chat with Mr. Miller."

"Right this way."

As I step inside his office and the door shuts gently behind me, I look around hesitantly. Am I alone? It's a little on the dark side, Mr. Miller's preference for artificial light quite apparent. Although he has windows, every blind is shut tightly. Wesley was right about the curtain. There, in the middle of the room, is a curtain the likes of which you would expect to see in a hospital room separating the different beds. The curtain completely conceals the desk on two sides, while the back and left sides of his secret area are barricaded by walls.

I head for the chair situated directly facing the curtained-off desk, but am halted.

"No, please, stay standing for a moment."

"Oh, hello. I'm sorry. I didn't realize you were in here."

"That's quite alright. Now, if you wouldn't mind, please turn around, slowly if you will."

"Excuse me?" I can't possibly have heard that correctly.

"Humor me. Just turn around. . . . slowly."

"You can see me?"

"Oh yes, very clearly."

"Uh, ok, but why do you want me to turn around?"

"My secretary has to be very pleasing to the eye. It's a prerequisite."

"You can't be serious. That's against the law."

"Don't worry. I don't tell the ugly applicants that."

Unable to believe my ears, I continue, "*You*, of all people, shouldn't judge a person by looks!"

"And why is that?"

"Um, well, you know . . . because of the accident and all."

Booming laughter fills the room. After he has settled down, he asks, "Is that what people are saying? That I've been in an accident?"

"Well, yes . . . haven't you?"

"I assure you that I haven't."

"Then why the curtain? Why don't you want people to see you?"

"Let's just say, I've been cursed with these looks since birth, but I certainly didn't have any traumatic accidents. I don't need my features distracting from my professional dealings. I prefer to conduct business in this fashion. Well?"

"Well, what? If you ask me, the curtain is far more distracting."

Chuckling, "I didn't ask you. Now, are you going to turn around for me, or is this interview over?"

"I'm not so sure I want to work for a pervert, Mr. Miller."

Again laughter drifts from behind the curtain.

"My sexual perversions run no deeper than voyeurism, Miss. . . . ?"

"It's Mrs. . . . just call me Miranda, thank you."

"Ok . . . Miranda. Due to my unusual circumstances, I allow nothing else. You have nothing to fear from me in that department. I will never lay a hand on you."

"Oh, my. You don't ever have sex?" Before I can stop myself, the words are blurted out and I turn several shades of crimson, horribly embarrassed. "I'm sorry. That was out of line."

"No more out of line than me asking you to turn around. No, I don't ever have sex. Now can you please take pity on my poor soul and allow me to see your full beauty?"

Feeling so sorry for this unfortunate and lonely man, I decide that allowing him to look at me isn't such a big deal. Hell, men look at women every day, and vice versa. What's the difference just because someone asks first?

"Ok, I'll turn around for you."

Slowly I begin to turn, yet, instead of feeling degraded, I feel more like I'm performing a kind act of charity. This is all this man ever gets. It's the least I can do for him. I resist the urge to offer to return every day, regardless whether or not I get the job.

"Thank you. Now please, have a seat."

"You're welcome."

As soon as I sit, I begin to fidget. This is right up there with my most strange experiences, and Lord knows, I've had my fair share.

"By the way, thank you for straightening out the lobby."

"Uh . . . oh . . . you're welcome. I was just passing the time."

Shit, how did he know that?. . . . I glance around nervously.

"I assume Wesley filled you in on the type of business we conduct here?"

"Yes, he did. A handyman service. I think it is a wonderful idea."

"Thank you. It does very well in areas such as this one . . . lots of wealthy divorcées. I would love to be able to incorporate women for hire as well, but there is more risk involved and not many women are willing to chance it. They assume that the men who hire them will expect sex."

"Hmmm . . . I can see that point. Do the men ever get asked for sex?"

"Not to my knowledge. However, I hear the tips are great."

"Oh. Then I suppose you only hire men that are pleasing to the eye as well?"

Chuckling, "I like your frankness, Miranda. Coincidentally, all of the men that work for me *are* rather good looking."

"I suspected as much. Anything else you'd like to tell me about?"

"Not for now. How about you? What is your work history? Are you currently employed?"

"No, I haven't worked in a few months. I had a pretty good career going, but decided it wasn't worth the stress."

"I see. Your application says you worked in a night club in California. Tell me about that."

I should have just left that off of the application.

"Oh, nothing much. It was just an odd job I stumbled upon to pay the bills. I mostly served cocktails."

"Interesting. With legs like yours, I would have figured you for a dancer."

Thunderstruck, I just about fall from my chair. Oh my God, he knows! He can't possibly know. Trying desperately to keep from hyperventilating, I struggle to regain my composure.

* * *

"Thank you," I manage to sputter out.

"Are you okay?"

"Yes, I'm fine . . . fine . . ."

"Well, let me explain what will be required of you if I offer and you accept this position. Of course, you'll be responsible for answering the phones and making appointments for the men. You'll also be expected to keep the lobby clean and coffee going, which I am already aware that you do quite well. The majority of your time will be spent attending to me."

"Just so there is no confusion, please define *attending*."

"I don't leave this office much during the day. I may need you to run errands for me, bring me coffee, and of course, be available for me to look at."

"Just look, right?"

"Just look."

"And how much do you intend to pay me for just looking pretty?" I ask, sarcastically.

"How does twenty dollars an hour sound to you?"

"Mr. Miller. You have yourself a deal, but at the first sign of any monkey business. . . ."

"You have my word, Miranda. You just make sure that you look your best each time you walk into this office."

"When would you like for me to start?"

"Can you finish out the day?"

"As a matter of fact, I can."

The remainder of the day passes without any glitches. Mr. Miller must have had his fill of looking, because he doesn't ask for me again. I basically have to teach myself the job, or more accurately, create the job. Since nothing has been set up beforehand, it is up to me to run the front desk how I see fit. Thrilled, I begin to organize the appointment book.

Each day is divided into twelve columns, and at the top of each column are the names of the handymen. The men all go by fictitious names, just in case one of the ladies gets too attached. Next, I review all of the messages on the answering machine, returning phone calls and setting up appointments. Each handyman has his own voice mail box where I am to leave and update all of his appointments. Once that is complete, I intercom Mr. Miller to ask if he needs anything else.

"No, thank you, Miranda. You've been a great help today already. It's almost five now. If you'd like, you can leave a little early. I'll see you back here at 9 AM sharp."

"Ok, then. Goodnight, Mr. Miller."

"Goodnight, Miranda."

I race home to fill Nick in on the events of my day only to be disappointed by his absence. Knowing that he will be home shortly, I pass the time checking my e-mail. Sure enough, another threatening poem is waiting for me.

Beware of where he goes . . .
For nobody ever knows . . .
Which day he'll plan to strike.
Beware of where you stand . . .
Cause you're putty in his hand . . .
He knows the things you like.

Darn it. Nick was supposed to speak to him about this. More annoyed than frightened, I quickly close the bothersome letter and move on to read the rest of my mail. There's one from Angela informing me that my VR suit is on the way and should be arriving in a day or two. Other than that, my box is disappointingly empty.

At dinner that night, I replay the events of the day for Nick to mull over.

"Mr. Miller does sound a bit weird. Be careful around him. Carry some mace or something."

"Don't worry. He promised me that all he wanted was to look, and that he would never attempt to touch me."

"Ah, my sweet. He does not know the power of your charms. He's doomed to break his promise . . ."

I positively purr, "Aw, Nick. I bet you say that to all your wives."

"Damn straight I do. Let's go upstairs. I'm feeling frisky. Shall we play a game?"

Giggling, I ask, "What's it to be tonight? French Maid? Airline Stewardess? Cave Woman?

"Nah, I think I want to see you dressed up all slutty, with me having to pay for it, no strings attached. I'm in the mood for the *streetwalker*."

"Oooo, baby. Let me go get ready."

Thirty minutes later, I descend the stairs looking like a harlot . . . cheap and tawdry but, ohhh so sexy. My hair is teased up big and poofy, held in place with industrial-strength hairspray. I went overboard on the makeup, painting my lips a sultry bright red, and adding false eyelashes for a more dramatic affect. I also couldn't leave out the authenticity of the moment, and doused myself with inexpensive perfume. The outfit I put together is just as sleazy, perfectly matching your typical stereotype prostitute. The fishnet stockings have a few extra holes in them, while my short, red, spandex skirt clings obscenely to the contours of my ass. I chose a black and red halter top accented with lace to complete the outfit, as well as a pair of five inch high, red spiked heels.

I strut in front of an appreciative Nick for several minutes before I turn to him and ask, "Looking for some action, sugah?"

"Wooooeee! How much is this action going to cost me?"

I answer his question while loudly chewing and popping my gum.

"Well, let's see. Depends on what you're looking for."

Slowly, I pull my gum out of my mouth and begin to twist it around my finger, the other end still clenched tightly between my teeth.

"What will twenty dollars get me?"

"Twenty dollars gets ya a blow job."

"Forty dollars?"

"Forty dollars gets ya straight sex, missionary position, no kink."

"One hundred dollars?"

I saunter over to him very suggestively and place my arms around his neck. "Sugah, for a hundred dollars, you can have whatever your little ole heart desires . . . for two straight hours."

"Anything?"

"Within reason of course. Just so long as you don't get carried away."

"Will you call me. . . . HumpDaddy?"

Unable to contain a snicker, I reply, "Oh, yes, but first, let's see the hundred."

Nick whips out a hundred dollar bill from his wallet. Without a moment's hesitation, I take the bill from him and stuff it into my cleavage, taking his hand and leading him up the stairs.

"Take me home, HumpDaddy. I've been a very naughty girl."

Before we even reach the top of the stairs, Nick's hands are all over me, fondling and groping anything he can catch hold of. He passionately kisses my entire face while whispering, "Oh, God, Randa. You look so fuck-ably nasty. I love it!"

"Now, now, big HumpDaddy. Settle down a bit. We want to be able to last the two hours, don't we?"

"That's not going to be a problem. Get in the bed-room."

Nick begins pulling devices out from all corners of the room. I watch in wide-eyed surprise as vibrators, whips, paddles, handcuffs and leather shackles go sailing through the air to land on the bed.

"Now, HumpDaddy, don't you go forgetting what I said about getting carried away. I'm seeing an awful lot of bondage and torture toys lying about."

Smiling, Nick explains, "Oh don't worry. We're going to do something different this time. I want *you* to tie *me*

---

up and be the dominant little slut. And these can be some of your accessories."

Grinning wickedly, I remark, "Well, well, well. It looks like *HumpDaddy* has been the naughty one. Come over to me this instant. And bring that cat-o-nine tails with you!"

"Yes, ma'am!"

Nick scurries to obey my order, thrilled that I'm jumping into the game with both feet. When he is standing before me, I yank the whip out of his grasp with one hand, while the other hand dives for his crotch.

"What do we have here, you naughty boy? I didn't say you could have an erection. You're going to have to be punished for this. Take off your clothes! Now!"

While Nick hurries to disrobe, I survey all of the goodies scattered about the bed. I select the few items that I'll need immediately, then return to face a naked Nick.

"Stand up straight! Put your hands behind your back! Nice. . . . very nice," I coo, as I walk around him to inspect my new plaything. Pinching his ass I say, "Oh, we're going to have some fun with this delectable piece of meat tonight. Did I mention that I like my steak rare and bloody?"

Before he has time to react to my question, I have his hands cuffed securely behind his back. I walk back around to face him and notice that his erect cock is twitching excitedly, and his pulse seems to have quickened.

*   *   *

"Ah, you like the thought of what I'm going to do to your ass, don't you? Now, spread your legs wide and keep them there."

Bending down, I fasten a spreader bar between and to his ankles. His legs are rendered helpless and immobile. Next comes the collar, a wide leather band with several silver spikes and loops jutting outward. Taking down the end of a chain already attached to the ceiling, I clamp it to one of the front loops on Nick's collar, tethering him to the ceiling.

"Oooo, my pet. I sure am enjoying the way you look all trussed up. It's just making my pussy all mushy inside."

Nick groans and rolls his eyes back into his head, totally enraptured by my nasty words.

"You like it when I talk dirty, don't you, my pet? Answer me!"

I raise the whip and bring it down sharply across Nick's erect penis.

"Ow, God damn it, Miranda. Not so hard."
"Oh, this will never do . . . never, never do."

I take from my pile of goodies, a penis gag and shove it into his protesting mouth, then affix it around the back of his head, compliments of the nifty velcro closure.

"Much better. Now I can dish out this part of your punishment without getting interrupted. Try not to move too much, lest you inadvertently choke or hang yourself," I warn.

Nick flinches as the whip comes down across his cock once again. Angrily, he tries complaining, but nothing other than muffled puffs of air are expelled. Again, WHACK.

"This is for getting an erection without permission." WHACK.

"This is for not getting undressed fast enough." WHACK.

"This is for not immediately answering my questions." WHACK.

"And this, is for speaking out of turn. You must always have my permission before you can speak. And you will address me as Mistress. Is that clear?" WHACK.

Nick nods his head as best he can in his tethered state and moans excessively trying to convey his understanding. By the last stroke of the whip, Nick's cock has sadly gone flaccid.

"Ok, you naughty boy . . . Now I'm going to whip your ass. You now have my permission to achieve an erection. But, first, let's get it all nice and ready."

Momentarily setting aside the whip, I reach for the baby oil and petroleum jelly. First, I pour a generous handful of the oil into my palm and rub my hands together. Next I begin to massage it onto Nick's tight buttocks. I take my time, savoring the feel of his clenching butt muscles, slipping a finger into the crack of his ass every so often, then reaching my hand down between his legs to cup his balls from the other side. When I am satisfied that his ass is well oiled, I dip a finger into the petroleum jelly and scoop some out. I move around so that I am perpendicular to his left side, his arm evenly dividing my breasts. My right leg and arm are behind him, and my left leg and arm are in front of him. I press up against him and grind my pubic bone into his hip as my left hand begins to massage his cock back to life and my right finger slowly works its way into his ass.

Nick begins to squirm and moan as my finger enters him deeper. His cock is back to a raging hard-on within seconds, and I continue with the hand-job as my finger fucks his ass.

"Does the naughty boy want to cum?"

"Mmmmpfff, mmmmmpffff, mmmmmpffff."

"Oh, that's too bad. The naughty boy can't cum. That would be a no-no."

Even as I am saying it, I don't relent in my stimulation of his genitals. I continue to work his cock and finger fuck his ass deeply until he groans and his cum is shooting out across the bedroom. Although thoroughly impressed, I pretend to be offended.

"You just can't help yourself, can you? What a bad, bad boy you are. I'm going to have to teach you a serious lesson."

I remove my finger from his ass and release my grip on his cock, then move behind him and pick up the whip. I begin to whip his shiny ass with much more force than

I used on his prick, until I hear him start to whimper. I move around to face him, surprised to see tears welling up in his eyes. Shit, I am going to be so dead once I let him go. . . .

"Has the naughty boy had enough?"

Nick answers with a murderous glare. Continuing on undaunted, I remark, "That expression doesn't look to me like you're the least bit sorry for your horrid behavior. I'm afraid we are going to have to continue your punishment, but I think I'll reposition you."

Unhooking his collar from the ceiling, I carefully push him backwards so that he is sitting at the foot of the bed. Then I remove the collar completely. Nick appears to breathe a sigh of relief.

"Ah, not so fast. I'm not done with you, pet. I want you to scoot back to the middle of the bed and then roll over so that you are lying down on your stomach. Then I'll release your hands."

Warily, Nick does as he is told, fully aware that I am still in possession of the whip. Patiently, he waits for me to make my next move. I take another pair of handcuffs out from the pile of goodies and connect a chain to it. Then I clamp one side of the cuffs to his right wrist, while connecting the chain to the headboard. I do the same with the cuffs that he is still wearing, chaining the left side to the headboard. Certain that he won't be able to get away, I unlock the cuffs holding both his wrists together. He attempts to break free, but is unsuccessful. Chastising him once again, I rearrange his arms so that they are now spread-eagled out in front of him and then shorten the distance of the chains locking his wrists to the headboard. I decide to leave his legs as is, nice and wide, held apart by the long metal bar.

"Let's see now. I bought you a new toy the other day. I think now is the perfect time to break it in. It's called a "cock taco" but I like to think of it as a "cockdog bun." It's so smooth and soft, flat and rubbery, perfect for cradling that naughty cock of yours while you're in this position. Now, I'll fill it with lots of lubricant so we can take your cock for the swim of its life. Lift your hips up, baby. That's it. Here you go. Now lower yourself down. How does that feel? Yummy?"

"Mmmmmmmmmmmmmmmmmmmmmmmmmmmmmm."

"Oh, yes. I thought you'd like that. Your cock surrounded in slick, slippery wetness. How does it feel when you squirm around?"

Nick rocks his body up and down to test the feeling.

"Mmmmmmmmm,Mmmmmmmmm,Mmmmmmmmmmm-mmmmmmmmmmmmmmm!"

"Perfect. Now every time I smack your ass, it will cause your dick to slide up and down, back and forth. Won't that be divine?"

Nick starts to make a racket, wiggling and squirming all over the place. Soon he has himself groaning as the wonderful sensations of his dick slipping through the lube register. Defeated, he stops and waits for the inevitable.

* * *

"I think I'll change to the paddle for the rest of your punishment. Twenty more swats ought to do it. One . . . SMACK . . . Two. . . . SMACK . . . Three. . . . SMACK. . . ."

Nick whimpers and gasps . . . then moans throughout the rest of his spanking. By the twentieth swat, he is humping away at the bed like a madman, trying to get the friction he needs to cum again. With one last thrill in mind. . . . I take one of my vibrators, grease it up, turn it on low, then place it under Nick's balls. Then I take a second vibrator, a bit larger, and really lube it up. Turning it up to high, I again begin to talk dirty to Nick.

"Oh, Nick. Now you're going to know how it feels to have a dick up your ass. I'm going to fuck you just like a woman, Nick. What do you think of that?"

I slowly start to insert the penis shaped vibrator into his ass. He begins bucking wildly. . . . stimulated fully in all areas. As his ass stretches to accept the entire length of the plastic shaft, I reach around to increase the speed of the vibrations under Nick's balls. Soon I am fucking his ass in time with his desperate thrusts against the "cock taco" still snuggled tightly beneath him. Repeatedly, I plunge the phallus into his ass, deeper and deeper. His moans are constant, grunting, groaning, wheezing, whimpering, until finally his whole body seizes into one big contraction. Convulsing into the sheets, Nick finally collapses and remains still.

"Nick? Are you okay? Nick?"

*　　*　　*

Oh God, I killed him. Worried that he is truly hurt, I hurry to release him. Finally, his arms are free and I quickly go to work on his legs. Once he is completely loose, I ask him again if he is alright. Slowly he rolls over onto his back, his belly a slimy mess, and looks up at me.

"Miranda, I'd beat you senseless except for that was the most fucking intense orgasm of my entire life."

The next minute, Nick is fast asleep.

CHAPTER 3

■

DEVIATIONS

"Miranda, can you please come see me in my office? I need to speak with you."

"Certainly, Mr. Miller," I reply into the intercom. "Can I bring you some coffee as well?"

"No thank you. Just your lovely self."

"I'll be right there."

I take a detour into the restroom to touch up my make-up. So far, Mr. Miller has been quite pleased at how flawless I've been keeping up my appearance. The last thing I need is to become complacent, jeopardizing my cush cush position here. And I thought dancing was easy money. Satisfied, I continue on down the hall and knock softly on Mr. Miller's door.

"Entre vous."

"Good morning, Mr. Miller. What can I do for you today?"

"Miranda. Come in and lock the door behind you. And

enough with the Mr. Miller formality. You can call me Beau."

Giggling, "Beau?" Unable to stop myself, I continue to snicker.

"May I ask why you find my name so humorous?"

"I'm sorry." I sputter out between my laughter. "It's just the way my mind works. I was just thanking God that your last name isn't Weevil."

Not amused, *Beau* asks me to have a seat.

"How long have you worked for me, Miranda?"

"After tomorrow, it will be two weeks, why?"

"Have you been enjoying your work here?"

"Immensely."

"Have you been enjoying my companionship as well?"

"Oh very much so. You are most interesting and entertaining."

"Hmmm . . . I was thinking the same of you . . . Anyway, have I, at any time, made you feel uncomfortable?"

"Other than my initial interview? No. I feel very comfortable in your presence."

"I'm glad to hear that. How does it make you feel to know that I'm watching you all the time?"

"Like I'm doing a good deed. . . ."

"Does it make you feel sexy?"

"Well . . . yes. I'm flattered that you selected me."

"Do you like to feel sexy?"

"What woman doesn't?"

"Do you like showing off your body for me?"

"Mr. Miller. . . ."

"Beau."

43

"Beau. Why are you asking me all of these questions? Now you are beginning to make me feel uncomfortable."

"I just want to know where your mind is before I ask you to do me another favor."

"What's the favor?"

"I purchased you some new clothes, ones that I would like for you to wear while you are alone with me."

"You're not happy with the ones I usually wear?"

"Oh, they're fine . . . acceptable. But they don't necessarily accentuate your figure as well as they could. What are you, about a size six?"

"Yes. Exactly, in most things, anyway. Sometimes a five, sometimes a seven, just depending on the style. You've got a pretty keen eye, Mr. Miller."

"Beau! Beau, Beau, Beau! My name is Beau. If you call me Mr. Miller one more time, Miranda, I'm going to have you thrashed!"

Tauntingly, I reply, "Ah, but, *Beau* . . . you promised never to lay a hand on me. You'd be breaking your promise."

"I never said I'd be doing the thrashing, Miranda. I'll just be watching. Don't be so smug."

"Ooookay then. How much skin do these new clothes reveal, *Beau*?"

"More than what you are accustomed to."

"Can I see the clothes before I make my decision?"

"Every day I'll have something new set aside for you to wear. You may decide at that time. If you choose not to wear them, then you are dismissed for the day."

"Uh, but you need me here. It doesn't make good business sense to send me home."

"No, it doesn't, but those are the conditions. Would you like to see what I have set aside for you today?"

"Do I have a choice?"

"Of course you have a choice, Miranda. You may leave for the day if you'd rather."

"No . . . no . . . no. Some choice. Where are the clothes?"

"They are in my private bathroom off the other end of my office. Remove all of your clothing and only put back on what I've set aside for you."

"I'm not saying that I'm agreeing to anything. I'm just willing to look at what you brought, that's all."

"Of course, Miranda. You'll find what you need in the bathroom."

I begin to sift through the delicate clothing stacked on the counter with trepidation. Everything is white. A white spandex dress with a white lace overlay, a white garter belt, a pair of white stockings with a white seam running up the back of each one, a pair of ridiculously high white heels, a white veil, and . . . Oh my God. A chastity belt.

What the hell? And why does it feel so deliciously kinky? For goodness sake, I wear less each time I visit the public swimming pool. Is it the idea, the symbolism that makes it feel so wrong, so twisted? As much as I try to reject the exquisite clothing, I can't resist the urge to try them on.

Several minutes later, I am completely decked out in my new costume, and the sight is breathtaking. Any woman would have looked just as devastating in such an outfit. Such pure, wanton sexual lust disguised in an aura of innocence. I still can't believe that I'm looking at my own reflection. I feel so beautiful, so provocative and so aroused. The dress, worn without a bra, is extremely tight, accentuating every curve. It is also so short that my cheeks hang out slightly, even standing as tall and straight as possible. The stockings only reach to mid thigh, hooked to the garter that continues up to eventually disappear beneath the dress. Loving the sight in front of me, I decadently run the palms of my hands up my rib cage to grasp and squeeze at my swollen breasts. I want to be ravished, right here, right now, in this outfit. Looking down, I notice the chastity belt still sitting suggestively on the counter. I pick it up and begin to examine it, never having seen one up close before. What an intimidating piece of equipment. Sighing, I slip it on and lock it up tight. God help me if I lose the tiny silver key. Adjusting the veil one last time, I prepare to make my entrance back into Beau's office.

I open the door quietly, still a little shy about what I'm doing. Hesitantly, I begin to walk toward his desk, unnerved by the suffocating silence.

"Stop. Don't move."

Startled, I freeze in my tracks. I stand for what seems like hours in dead silence, unsure of what to do.

"Beau?"

"Shhhhh. Just stand there. I've died and gone to heaven."

Relieved that he likes what he sees, I begin to relax as I innocently pose for him.

*   *   *
———

"Can a slut be a virgin? That's what you look like. A virginal slut . . . a virginal slut nurse to be exact. Turn around and face the wall. I want to look at your backside for a while."

My pulse quickens at his words as I slowly turn back to face the direction of the bathroom. Oh God, I moan, as a warm gush of fluid rushes down to settle in the bottom of the chastity belt.

"You are stunning, Miranda. Lift the bottom of your dress up a little higher. Please? Just a little higher. Why hide such a beautifully round and sexy ass? Show it to me."

Swooning, I do as I'm told, enjoying the display almost as much as he. As I hike my dress up a couple more inches, another wave of moisture finds its way down into my chastity belt. I hear Beau groan from behind the curtain as he begins to fumble around.

"Oh, yesssss. Now spread your legs wide and lean over . . . just a little. Oh yes, just like that. Stay like that. Oh, Miranda. I'm taking my cock out and I'm going to masturbate while I look at you. Does that turn you on to know that I'm back here, beating my meat, all on account of you? Huh, can you hear it? Can you hear my hand sliding up and down my cock? Can you hear how fast I'm pumping it, Miranda. Oh, yesss. Oh, God, yessss . . . I'm going to cum in a minute. I'd love to spurt my seed all over that ass, but I made you a promise, didn't I? Ohhh, Ohhh, Ohhh yeah, yeah, yeah. Wiggle your ass for me. Sway it gently back and forth. Ummmm, yessss, just like that. What a peach. I'd love to take a bite out of that peach. Just a little longerrrrrr. I can feel my balls boiling, Miranda. I'm getting ready . . . ready. . . . Ah . . . ah . . . ahhhhhhhhhhhhhhhhhhhhhh . . . AAAAAHHHHHHHRRRGGGGGGGGG!!!

Flushed, I stand there, swaying, barely able to keep on my feet. I am so wet and horny, dying to be fucked. Oh God, I wish Nick were here. I'm half inclined to beg Quasimodo to come have his way with me, needing desperately to assuage the ache that has begun spreading.

"You're horny, aren't you? I can hear your tiny whimpers. You'd give anything to be able to touch yourself right now, wouldn't you, Miranda? And that mean, nasty belt is in your way. Tomorrow. Tomorrow we're going to do this again, but tomorrow there won't be any belt. Tomorrow you're going to masturbate and get yourself off for me, isn't that right, Miranda?"

"Yes . . . yes . . . whatever you say. . . ."

Just then a steady three knocks sound out as the door to Beau's office flies open.

"Mr. Miller, I . . . "

"For God's sake, Dante! I'm in the middle of something. Close the door immediately!"

I turn to look over my shoulder, mortified that someone should catch me in such a compromising position. My horror intensifies as my gaze takes me directly to the brilliant sky blue eyes of none other than my tormentor, Russ. Squealing, I yank my dress back down to cover my bottom as I stand to confront him. His face registers bewilderment, then shock, then amusement . . . and then pure evil.

---

* * *

"Dante, remain inside and close the door please."

Dante?

"Well, if Miranda had locked the door like I had asked her to, we could have avoided this little bit of embarrassment. Dante, I'd like for you to meet Miranda. She started working here about two weeks ago as our receptionist. Miranda, this is Dante, one of my handymen."

Unable to speak, I just gape at Russ. Russ, highly amused, informs Mr. Miller that we already know each other, quite well, in fact. Oh God, no, Russ. Please don't tell him about the poker game. I shake my head and silently plead with him not to say another word. He just continues to grin. Never have I wished more fervently for a swift and painless death as in this moment.

"I apologize for interrupting you, Mr. Miller. I didn't realize that you weren't alone. I'll let you get back to . . . uh, whatever it was you were doing. My problem can wait."

Snickering, Russ gleefully leaves the office. Shattered, I slump down into the chair waiting for Beau to let me have it.

"Miranda, you have put me in a very bad position. Why didn't you lock the door when I asked you to?"

"I think I got sidetracked . . ."

"Yes, you were too busy laughing at my name, as I recall, to follow a simple instruction! I'm absolutely livid. I have half a mind to fire you on the spot!"

"Go ahead. That's the least of my worries at the moment. I can't work here knowing that Russ works here too."

"Dante could make serious trouble for me if he wanted to because of your carelessness. You're not getting off that easily. You *will* continue to work here, even if it means I have to share you with him to keep him quiet."

"NOOOOOOO! God, no! You can't do that! And his name is Russ. Stop calling him Dante! It's driving me crazy."

"Miranda, you need to calm down and get a hold of yourself. I'm the one in jeopardy here. Pour yourself a drink. I have liquor in the cupboard above the filing cabinets. I need to think for a moment."

Needing no further encouragement, I bolt for the liquor and begin to slam down shots of tequila. After the third one, I pause to catch my breath, just in time for the nasty taste to hit me as zillions of shivers consume my body. Ok . . . that was stupid . . . and I slowly wander back to the chair.

"How do you know Russ?"

"Huh?" I ask, alarmed.

"Why can't you work here if Russ works here? What's up between the two of you?"

"It's a long story, one I'd rather not tell, if you don't mind."

"I do mind. I'm directly involved now. My company is at stake. I need to know. If you don't tell me, I'll get the story from Russ, and I'm sure he'll paint a different picture."

Defeated, I spend the next ten minutes explaining to Beau the events leading up to, during and after the poker game, as well as informing him about the threatening poems being sent to my e-mail.

"My, my, my. I do believe I am seeing you in a different light. But, I do understand the problem now."

Then, without warning, he bursts out laughing.

"I'm sorry, Miranda. I know this is serious, that he's threatened to harm you, but of all the people to walk in on us and catch you with your ass hanging out like that. It's too . . . too . . . much!"

"Laugh all you want, but it isn't funny. I'm gonna be sick."

I stand up to leave, heading in the direction of the bath-room.

"Where are you going?"

"I'm changing, and then I'm going home."

"Wait, wait. Don't be so hasty. I promise you I'll take care of things. You won't have to worry about running into Russ. I'll make sure he stays very busy . . . and dis-tracted. Now, please make sure the door is locked so that we don't get interrupted again."

"It's locked, but I'm not in the mood to play anymore. I want out of these clothes."

"Well, Miranda, *I* still do want to play. You have no

idea how sexy you look right now in your disarray. Let's just forget this whole incident ever happened. Have another shot of tequila."

Shivering, I politely decline, as the warmth from the first three shots slowly begins to seep magically into my bloodstream. The affect is calming, and soon I am relaxed and accepting, no longer intent on fleeing.

"Open the bottom drawer of my filing cabinet. It's locked, but the key is in it."

I open the drawer suspiciously, and with good cause. Inside I find an extensive array of sexual toys, ranging from handcuffs to rope, from dildos to paddles.

"You sure have quite the collection of kink for somebody that never has sex," I comment as bravely as possible. What have I gotten myself into?

"There are many ways of achieving sexual gratification, Miranda. Take out the pair of handcuffs with all the fur around them."

"What do you want me to do with them?"

"Put them on. Not too tightly, but tight enough so that your wrists can't slide out of them."

"You're scaring me. I'm beginning to think I don't know you at all."

"You have nothing to be afraid of. I promised not to touch you and I won't. I like the way a woman looks when she's bound and helpless. The key will remain within your reach to unlock when the time comes."

"Do you promise that you're not going to invite Russ back once I'm vulnerable?"

"I promise. If I had known about Russ earlier, I never would have threatened to share you with him. That was anger talking. I'm truly not *that* wicked."

"Okay, the cuffs are on as tightly as I feel comfortable making them."

"Just set the key on top of the filing cabinet and then step back into the middle of the room."

A strange noise directly behind me causes me to jump as I toss the key down and search for the source. There, being lowered from the ceiling by a thick chain, appears to be a mini trapeze bar with a metal clasp on the bottom of it.

"Hook the middle of your cuffs to the clasp at the bottom of that bar, and then face me. Now, grab the bar. You're going for a ride."

Slowly the chain begins to recede back into the ceiling, pulling my arms up with it. Soon I am on my tip toes, grasping the bar for dear life. The chain stops, momentarily.

"I also like the way a lady looks when she's all stretched out. Very fetching, indeed. How do you feel?"

"Probably the way you want me to feel. I'm not comfortable, if that's your point."

Laughing, he informs me, "This is going to be your resting position. And this. . . ."

The chain begins to move upward again until my feet are no longer touching the floor.

" . . . is how you'll hang for the remainder of the time. When your hands get tired of holding onto the bar, you can let go and dangle from your cuffs. When your arms start to hurt from holding your body weight, then you can grab hold of the bar again. And, when I think you need a break, I'll lower your feet back onto the floor for a small rest."

"Why are you doing this?"

"Because it pleases me. . . . and because I'm still pissed that you left the door unlocked. I wasn't going to show you that drawer for a couple more weeks, but the admission of the types of situations you were involved with in that poker game led me to believe that you were ready now."

Groaning . . . my arms already beginning to protest, "What . . . I'm not as sweet and pure as you had first thought?"

"Your face is deceiving. Very wide, expressive, innocent brown eyes. And your body screams, 'fuck me,' leaving me with quite a challenge on my hands. How many times since you've started working here have you wondered what it would be like to fuck me?"

Gasping, shocked, "What kind of a question is that?"

"A very straight forward one. Now I'd like an honest answer to it."

"I imagine you horribly disfigured. What makes you think I've thought about it even once?"

"I'd bet my life on it. Now, how many times?"

Struggling, my grip starting to weaken, I beg, "Please let me down. My arms are getting sore."

"Not yet, my sweet. You don't know the meaning of sore. How many times?"

"God damn it! You're beginning to tick me off!"

"Temper, temper. How many times?"

During my struggles, I manage to somehow get myself twirling slowly in a clockwise position. Finally my hands give up and I feel a mild jerking in my shoulders as the burden of my weight is transferred. It doesn't take long before I feel the cuffs digging into my wrists, despite all the padded softness of the fur.

"Please, let me down. This hurts."

"Answer my question and I'll let you down for a while."

"Okaaay . . . Once, just once," I practically whine.

"When?"

"Uhhh . . . please! . . . Today . . . in the bathroom . . . when I first put on the outfit. I wanted so much to be fucked in this outfit."

Immediately, the chain begins to lower until I feel my toes touch the floor. He stops the chain so that I have to remain on tiptoes, even in the outrageous heels. Relief floods through me as my arms begin to relax a little, my legs now carrying the load.

"You wanted to be fucked by me?"

"I wanted to be fucked by anybody. You were just the closest. I was actually hoping for my husband."

"Tell me about your husband."

"Can you lower me a little more, please, so that I'm not on my tiptoes?"

"In a moment. When your thighs start to quiver and shake."

"Damn, you're a bastard. . . ."

"Careful, I can hoist you right back up there . . ."

"Why do you want to know about my husband?"

"Just curious. What is he like?"

"Well, he's only the most perfect man on the face of the planet. Perfect *person* to be exact."

Chuckling, "Well, it's obvious you adore him. What makes him so perfect?"

"I don't know, exactly. It's kind of like his sole purpose in life is to please me. Everything he does is with respect to how it will affect me. I didn't ask him to be that way. He just is, and sometimes I feel so guilty, like I don't deserve him. But it makes *him* happy to be that way, so I guess we both win. Like I said, he's perfect."

"Does he satisfy you sexually?"

"Oh, God, yes. Satisfying me sexually is what he lives for."

"That must be quite a job, satisfying a nymphomaniac."

"That's not fair. I'm not a nympho."

"Oh, no? What would you call yourself?"

"I'm. . . . just. . . . very sexually aware, that's all."

"So sexually aware that he has to share you with his friends to keep you satisfied? I'd call that a nymphomaniac . . . "

"It's not like that. He doesn't *have* to share me with his friends. He wants me to be able to live out as many of my sexual fantasies as I can. He realizes that some fantasies he just cannot fulfill. That's why he staged the poker game. Not because he had to."

"He's a very generous man. If you were mine, I don't think I'd want to share you."

"He's just very secure and knows it is only he who

holds my heart. No matter what happens, I'll always come home to him."

"Does he know about me?"

"Yes. I told him that I was hired because you found me attractive and wanted to spend your days looking at me."

"Are you going to tell him about today? By the way, how *are* your legs faring?"

"They're shaking quite nicely, thank you. Care to let me down?"

Beau lowers the chain another inch or two, allowing my whole body time to recover. My arms are still stretched above my head, but not pulled tightly.

"Oh, thank you. I've learned not to keep any secrets from my husband. I'll tell him about today."

"Hmmm. I hadn't counted on that. Will he come after me?"

"No. He'll get me to admit that I was turned on by the whole experience and then fuck my brains out."

Laughing, "Your husband sounds like a man after my own heart. I do believe I would like to meet him someday."

"Would he get to see your face?"

"Nah, I'm afraid not. Nobody gets to see my face. Not yet, anyway. Perhaps someday."

"I'm sure you're not as ugly as you think you are. You *sound* handsome."

"Charming . . . A modern day Beauty and the Beast. Perhaps if you kissed me, I'd change into a handsome prince? Ah, a man can dream. . . ."

"I would kiss you, you know, if I thought it would help. You could blindfold me."

"I don't want your kisses of pity, Miranda, but the offer is sweet. Now, I think you've had a long enough rest, time to hoist you back up. Hold on."

"Uuhhhhhhh . . . "

I spend the remainder of the day hanging in limbo. Beau continues to ask me questions about my life and my relationship with Nick. He masturbates twice more, both times while I am hanging and pleading with him to release me. He finally allows me down for good around 4:30, reminding me before I leave for the day what he promised would happen tomorrow.

On my way out the door, I feel a tug on my arm and turn to see a grinning Russ.

"Mind if I walk you home?"

"Hell, yes, I mind. Leave me alone, will you?"

I continue walking, picking up the pace, making sure I stay well out in the open. Russ wouldn't dare make a move with all these people as witnesses. Russ continues to walk right alongside me and starts to singsong:

"You should finish what you start . . .
Cause you know deep in your heart . . .
That you crave a wild conclusion.
Such a shameless, pretty face . . .
Shall be put back in its place . . .
To avoid any confusion."

*　　*　　*

"Damn it, Russ. Stop that!"

"That was a mighty pretty sight I walked in on this morning. Are you doing Mr. Miller?"

"No, I'm not *doing* Mr. Miller. He just likes me to dress up for him. You know he's deformed."

"So I've heard. So, how come you'll play with everybody but me?"

Russ grabs my arm and turns me to face him.

"Let. . . . Go . . . Of. . . . My. . . . Arm! If you try anything, so help me God, I'll scream my head off."

Angrily,

"The time just isn't right . . .
Though I do enjoy the sight . . .
Of your sweet lips as they quiver.
Turn around and walk away . . .
But the sight of me today . . .
Will leave you cold to shiver."

Russ thankfully stomps off in the opposite direction.

"Nick! You are never going to believe the day I had."

CHAPTER 4

■

EXPLORATIONS

"Miranda. A package just came for you."

"Is it from Angela?" I ask, expectantly.

"No, but it is from Mexico. Isn't Angela's friend from Mexico?"

"Yes! Yes! That's got to be it! Give it here!"

I tear open the package and examine the contents inside very carefully. The first thing I remove is the head gear. It looks mostly like a pair of goggles and headphones with a very extensive mouth and chin piece. All in all, it's quite light and non-cumbersome. What I pull out next resembles a ski mask, all in black with holes cut out for the eyes, ears, mouth and nostrils. It is made of an extremely luxurious, suede-like material, making it very pleasing to hold against my face. At the bottom of the neck are connectors, which I assume must fasten to the rest of the suit. The suit itself is made of the same material as the ski mask, and all one piece including the gloved hands and feet, zipping closed in the front. It reminds me of something "Catwoman" would wear, very sleek and sexy, except for the fact that the entire crotch area is missing and tiny connectors are visible around the edges.

I dig deeper into the box and find the missing crotch piece. It is made of sturdier material, more like that of the head gear, and it is quite clear how it works. There are two very distinctive "nubs" which are to be placed directly on the vaginal and anal openings, then the device can be fastened to the rest of the suit by the connectors. Well? It is a sex suit, after all . . . and the piece is removable, making sex in VR optional. I don't *have* to wear it.

The very last item I remove from the box appears to be a swing, a very strange looking swing. It looks more like what you would wear if you were jumping out of an airplane, what the parachute is attached to, only no parachute.

"Ok, Nick. Here are the instructions. Want to help me set it up?"

Two hours later, the swing is in place and the software installed. Apparently, when in VR, you need to be safely secured in the swing to avoid injuring yourself. Nick installed the swing to tilt backwards, so that when I am sitting in it, I will be comfortably reclining. Eager to begin, I ask, "Now what? I just can't go in there, can I? Don't I need to set up a time so that I am not all by myself?"

"Probably. Why don't you send Angela an e-mail letting her know that you're already to go and see what you need to do from here."

_____

<Poseidon>	Hello, Aphrodite.
<Aphrodite>	Hello there. Where did you come from?

"Nick, come look at this!"

<Poseidon>	This is the Virtual Reality chat room which automatically activates when your computer goes online. It was installed when you downloaded the VR software. This is where we arrange our VR scenarios.
<Aphrodite>	How many others besides Angela and I have suits?
<Poseidon>	Yours is the 20th.
<Aphrodite>	Are the suits working the way they're supposed to? Have you had any problems?
<Poseidon>	A glitch here and there, all of which have been worked out. My "guinea pigs" are thrilled with their VR experiences.
<SeaNymph>	Hey you two!
<Aphrodite>	Angela! Hi there. I have my suit. I'm already to go. Have you tried it yet?
<SeaNymph>	No, I've been waiting for you.
<Poseidon>	Would you ladies like to try it now?
<SeaNymph>	Sure, I'm game.
<Aphrodite>	Me too. I'd like it short and sweet though, so I can test the waters. And I most definitely don't want to experience sex my first time in Virtual Reality. Can we make it nice and platonic?
<Poseidon>	Absolutely. Where would you like to

		meet? As you can see when you open up the VR program, it gives you a list of locations. Choose one.
<SeaNymph>	I	Randi, you party pooper! Antonio, I'm still game for sex. I'll be wearing my crotch attachment.
<Poseidon>	I	Ah, Angela. You're shameless. That's what I love about you. Even in platonic VR, I would still highly recommend wearing your "crotch" attachment, as Angela so eloquently put it. Otherwise, it could get a bit drafty, not to mention, if you change your mind, you'll have to exit the program to go and retrieve it.
<SeaNymph>	I	Well, what's it called then?
<Poseidon>	I	It's simply called the "sex insert."
<Aphrodite>	I	I kind of like the looks of the private yacht for a location. What about you, Angela? Any preferences?
<SeaNymph>	I	Oooo, that sounds heavenly to me. Antonio?
<Poseidon>	I	The private yacht it is then ladies! How about if I have us sailing around the Hawaiian Islands?
<Aphrodite>	I	Oh my God . . . this is sooo cool. I can't wait.
<Poseidon>	I	In 15 minutes, I'll have the program ready to go. You can access it any time after that just by clicking your mouse on the location icon. Then, take your place in the swing and put on the head gear. There is a small knob above the right ear which activates the helmet. Turn it on

and then sit back and enjoy the experience. See you soon.

Oh my goodness. I can't believe it's actually going to happen.

"Do you think you'll need any help getting into this suit?"

"Yeah, stick around and make sure I do this right, ok?"

The suit is tricky, but is soon on and fitting like a glove. Each finger and toe are wrapped snugly in their own little section of the suit, as well as my breasts being sucked up into the built-in bra cups. Next I slip on the "sex insert," making sure that the two little nubs are well lubricated before I clamp them so near and dear to my delicate openings. I wriggle around a bit, enjoying the feel of the sturdy piece between my legs. Next, I pull back my hair and slip the hood over my face. Nick helps me by attaching the neck to the rest of the suit. Oh, God. Almost time.

"Why don't you go get comfortable in the swing? I'll click on the location when it's time."

"Ok, but I'm a little scared. You won't let anything happen to me, will you?"

"Of course not. Want to set a time limit? I'll exit you from the program at that time if you haven't come out on your own."

"Yeah, let's do that. Just in case. How about 30 minutes?"

"Ok. If you're not back in 30 minutes, I hope you're not doing something fun when I shut you down!"

Laughing, "For your information, I'm keeping my first VR experience G-rated!"

"Okay, but I know women. They're famous for changing their minds!"

"I'll risk it."

I climb up into the swing and relax.

"Ah, this is nice! I feel weightless."

I let my legs dangle freely as I lie back into the comfortable back support.

"I could stay in this all day! We need to get you one. They'd be great outside, even better than a hammock."

"Well, don't fall asleep and miss all the fun . . ."

"Has it been 15 minutes yet?"

"Yup, 17 to be exact. Want me to fire it up?"

"Yeah, but come give me a kiss first, just in case I come out of this and my brains are scrambled. I may not recognize you."

"I doubt that . . . but I'll kiss you anyway, assuming I can find your lips around all that mask."

"They're right here. See? They have to be accessible . . . you know, so that I can talk . . . and stuff."

"It's the. . . .'and stuff' that I want to know about!"

"I promise to tell you all about it. Now come give me that kiss."

After Nick kisses me and clicks on the yacht icon, I don my headpiece carefully, making sure my headphones are directly over my ears, and my mouth is placed flat up against the mouth piece. With a few minor adjustments, the helmet is on snug and secure. Taking a deep breath, I cautiously turn the knob over my right ear.

Immediately, soothing music begins playing in the headphones, helping me to relax, while my eyes behold a subtly increasing hue of swirling colors. Soon the music changes to the sounds of birds and a startling bright blue dominates my vision. I get the sensation that I'm flying as I begin to see the birds that I have been hearing, and white puffy clouds splattered sparingly throughout the wide expanse of blue sky. The sun is brilliant, and I can feel it slowly warm my body as I continue my journey. No longer afraid, I begin to move and turn my head in all directions, marveling at this incredible experience. Even if VR went no further than this, I would be thrilled just knowing what it feels like to fly. Thank you, Angela.

I can see the yacht that I assume I'll be "landing" on sitting prettily alongside one of the Hawaiian Islands. Everything is so colorful, the vegetation lush and green, fruit so ripe I can almost taste it, and the smells. . . . ah, I can smell everything. Clean, crisp, fruity, earthy and moisture. As I float closer to the ship, I can hear the ocean, hear the waves as they crash against the surf, watching the impressive yacht bob up and down with each passing wave. It's incredible, and so easy to forget that I'm not actually here.

I hold my arms out in front of me, taking on the "Superman" pose, expecting to see my gloved fingers, and become startled by the sight of flesh. What I see are my very own hands, with one heck of a nice manicure, nails painted a pale pink. My wedding and engagement

---

rings are right where they belong, as well as the class ring that I wear constantly on my right, middle finger. This is too much . . . Every last detail appears to be taken into account. Amazed, I continue to gaze at my hands, flipping them over and over until I decide to take the real test. Apprehensively, I take my right index finger and stroke it along the inside of my left palm. I feel it! I can feel the soft, tickling sensation, and decide to add more pressure to see if the sensation changes. Thrilled to find that it does, I scratch at my palm with my nails. Not only is the sensation accurate, I begin to notice a slight reddening of my palm and a mild burning from my curious abuse.

Forgetting my hands for the moment, I concentrate on where I am being taken. I am getting very close to the ship, serenely afloat and picturesque in the tropical setting. Although I see and hear many things, none of them are human. I haven't seen any people, on the island or on the ship—no cars, no traffic, nothing to disrupt the peaceful tranquility of the setting. It's positively heavenly. Who needs a vacation when there is VR?

The landing on deck is very gentle, like I had been placed there by a set of invisible arms, very controlled and steady. Looking around, I see that I am at the back of the yacht and all alone. The deck is beautiful, with a built in swimming pool occupying at least one-third of the space, surrounded by a few lounge chairs and umbrella'd tables. At the very end is a cocktail bar decorated as a Tiki hut, complete with a grass roof.

*　　*　　*

I walk around and begin to touch things, comparing them to the real world. I touch a table, drag my fingers through the water in the pool, move a chair and then walk on over to the bar. I begin to notice that my feet are getting warm and look down to see that I am indeed, barefoot. I also notice for the first time that I can see my bare legs and most of my body, covered in nothing but a skimpy pink swimming suit. Smiling, I turn to head back toward the center of the ship, hoping to find Angela.

"AYYYYYYYEEEEE," I screech, very unladylike. "You scared me!"

Chuckling, the handsome man extends his right hand and introduces himself.

"I apologize, Miranda. I did not mean to startle you. I am Antonio. It's a pleasure to finally meet you."

"You, as well. Whew, it's going to take me a minute or two to get my wits back together. I was beginning to think I was all alone on this ship."

"I'm a little mischievous that way," Antonio replies. "I like to watch people when they think they are by themselves. But I truly didn't mean to frighten you."

"Mmmmm Hmmmm. I'm not so convinced."

"Since we have some time to kill waiting for the others, would you like for me to show you around the yacht?"

"Sure, that would be wonderful."

I take a few minutes to size up my host as he busies himself with the grand tour. Now that my nerves are back in check, I am able to really get a good look at him. I was expecting more of a "Mr. Ruark—Welcome to Fantasy Island" type of man, not something right out of Playgirl magazine. He appears to be in his early to mid thirties, not so much because of his looks, but more from his air of confidence. It's quite obvious, too, that he either comes from or has access to lots and lots of money. He is about six feet tall, with a strong and healthy appearance, not overly muscular, but very sinewy. Black loose curls adorn his head and neck, tapered to lay gracefully between his shoulders. His eyes are killer, a deep jade green, almost teal at times, and they possess a naturally lazy bedroom droopiness to them. His nose is very aristocratic and his lips have that puffy "kiss me" look to them. Overall, his looks are almost too perfect, too pretty, but with just one smile, I can see how he could charm the pants off of anything. . . . man or woman. This man is way too sexy for anyone's good. Angela will positively drool when she meets him.

"And this is your stateroom. Would you like some time to freshen up before Angela arrives?"

"She'll be here soon, right? I can only stay for thirty minutes. My husband is going to disconnect the program if I take any longer. We set that up in advance, just as a precaution."

"I understand. She should be here any time, but even if you get plucked from the program, you can always return. Speaking of which, there are several pull stations that look like fire alarms located in every section of this ship. If at any time you want to exit, just pull one of them. It immediately disables your headgear."

"That's good to know. Thanks, I'll only be a minute. Where should I meet back up with you?"

"By the pool is fine. Now, let's see if I can go sneak up on Angela!"

With a wink, Antonio disappears and I am left standing in complete luxury. Only the gentle rocking of the room reminds me that I am not in the Presidential Suite at a 5-star hotel. Everything is decorated in gold and white, from the comforter of the king-size bed to the fixtures in the bathroom. There is a sliding glass door leading to a balcony overlooking the edge of the ship and into the pristine waters below. The mirror is what I am most concerned with at the moment, dying to get a peek at what I look like in VR.

Whoa! I've never looked so good. I'm sure Antonio must have shaved a couple of pounds off as he recreated my image in VR. Turning, I'm pleased to see that not an ounce of cellulite exists at the tops of my thighs, while my breasts seem to have increased a cup size. My face is flawless . . . not a wrinkle, not a blemish— smooth, even color. I wipe my hand against my cheek to see if it's covered with makeup, but nothing comes off. No wonder he looks so pretty. He can fine-tune any flaw or even make it disappear. I love the little pink suit that he had picked out for me, and satisfied with my appearance, return to the pool deck.

Quickly, I duck back around the corner and out of sight as my brain registers the intimate scene I had just unwittingly intruded upon. Angela is there alright, but must have been very anxious to try out her sex insert. Embarrassed, yet too curious to stop myself, I slowly steal another peak around the corner. Oh my God . . . to witness such unleashed passion, so beautiful, so erotic. Angela and Antonio are completely nude, the remains of

Angela's suit piled carelessly at her feet. The sun is beating off of their already hot and sweaty bodies as they continue to thrash and kiss torridly. Finally Antonio has Angela backed up against the Tiki Bar and pushes her down backwards to lie across it, wrapping her legs around his waist. Without any further preliminaries, Antonio inserts himself and begins to thrust into Angela like a wild man. I watch in awe as the strong muscles of his ass flex with each savage plunge, suddenly wishing that I could trade places with her.

My God. . . . how can such a primitive coupling as this be so artistic? I can't tear my gaze away! I've never seen such a fierce and frenzied assault as this, and Angela appears to be loving every minute of it. Such a contrast to hear her sweet melodious voice screaming. . . . "Fuck me harder, you bastard! Oh, God, Yes, Antonio! Yes! Hurry . . . I'm there! YYYYEESSSSSS!" Antonio shouts out his own release, only in a language that I'm not at all familiar with. Still, it sounds so hot and sexy, my own blood begins to boil.

Breathing heavily, I close my eyes and lean back against the wall, no longer spying on the rutting couple and wishing I had never seen it. How can I face them now, especially when all I can think about is receiving the same ravishing treatment from Antonio myself? I'm going to have to get out of here and back to Nick, and soon.

As soon as I open my eyes, I again almost scream as I find myself nose to nose with none other than Antonio. His hand quickly covers my mouth to stifle any noise, and makes a shushing sound. Convinced that I have recovered from my shock, he removes his hand.

"How . . . ? Angela. . . . ? But . . . ?"

"Spying is not very nice. Just wait till I tell my brother. . . ."

"What . . . ? Who . . . ? Oh God . . . "

Smiling, he enlightens me. "I'm Lucas, Antonio's twin brother. He asked me to keep you company if he and Angela got carried away and neglected you. It looks like they're working on it, doesn't it?"

"Um. . . . I think it was just poor timing on my part. I think . . ."

"Did you get off watching them? They are a sexy couple, I'll have to admit."

"Did I get off?. . . . How long were you watching me?!?"

"Long enough," he grins wickedly.

"You must be the evil twin. . . ." I whisper under my breath.

"What was that?"

"Nothing. Shall we go join the lovebirds?"

"Hmmm . . . let's give them a few more minutes to get themselves together. Besides, I'm more interested in getting to know you."

"I'm married. Sorry to dash your hopes."

Lucas begins to laugh and then completely falls into hysterics.

"What is sooo funny?"

"This is VR, baby. You can't be unfaithful in VR! It's not even really happening. For instance, when I touch your bottom lip with my thumb, it's not really happening."

I feel a sudden, electric jolt as Lucas touches my lip . . . an all-too-familiar sensation that seems to be directly connected with my already over eager sex.

"Or, when I slip your bikini straps off of your shoulders . . . it's not really happening."

Oh God, here we go. Goosebumps rise as he slowly drags the straps and his fingers across my shoulders and down my arms. Moaning internally. . . .

"Or when I kiss the hollow of your throat, it's not really happening. . . ."

Whimpering, I get lost in the warm wetness from his mouth and tongue on my throat, moving slowly further and further down. Lucas stops at my nipple, still covered by the swimsuit top, and then takes a frisky nip at it, softly grinding it between his teeth.

"Ouch!"
"And that didn't really happen either."

As he straightens himself back to his full height, he doesn't pass up the opportunity to swipe the entire right side of my face with the length of his long, wet tongue.

"Pretty tasty for something not really here."

A scream from the deck momentarily distracts us as we both rush in the direction of the pool. We are just in time to see Antonio hoisting Angela up into his arms to throw her into the swimming pool. Another scream follows as she goes sailing through the air to become submerged. Lucas, not about to be undone by his brother, follows suit, and soon I am gasping and choking in the pool right alongside Angela. Thrilled to finally see one another again, Angela and I hug and start chatting, totally willing to forgive the boys for the unmerciful dunking.

For the next ten minutes, we all make ourselves comfortable on the lounge chairs, mine positioned between Angela and Lucas, while Antonio lies peacefully on the other side of Angela. Amazingly, ten minutes is all Angela and I need to catch up on everything, which is perfect since my thirty minutes of VR are just about up. Begrudgingly, I glance over at Lucas as I say my goodbyes, just in time to catch him stroking himself through his swimming trunks. He grins suggestively as he continues to play with his impressive erection. "It'll be waiting for you when you get back, baby."

Oh God, what a pig! "Don't hold your breath, Lucas. Ok, Antonio, how do I get out of here?"

As if by magic, everything disappears and I am groggily brought back to my basement and Nick.

After removing the headgear, I smile at my husband and say, "Oh, Nick. That was so awesome. We need to get you a suit!"

"Did you get lucky? You were moaning and groaning there for a while."

Blushing, I explain, "Well, not really. But it was close. Antonio has a brother."

"Ah, say no more!"

Giggling, I relate every tiny detail of my VR experience to Nick, from the thrill of flying to the feel of a thick, wet tongue against my cheek.

CHAPTER 5

■

PERVERSIONS

"I'm pleasantly surprised to see you today. I thought for sure I scared you away."

"Well, if I had any sense at all, I'd quit this job. But my curiosity always gets the better of me. Hate to think I might miss anything. . . ."

"Did you remember to lock the door today?"

"Oh, yes. That's a mistake I won't make twice."

"Hmmm, I may have to find another reason to string you up, then. I found that far too arousing to do only once."

"Please, not too often. My body is still sore."

"That only excites me more . . . when you beg. Let me outline for you what's going to happen today. This first hour, I'll actually let you get caught up with your work. Make sure all the appointments are scheduled and calls returned. Then, for the remainder of the day, you will stay in my office and masturbate for me."

"All day?" I ask, incredulous.

"Yes, all day. How many times do you think you can cum in seven hours, Miranda?"

"Uh . . . I don't know. I never tried it before."

"Well, I'm hoping for ten, expecting seven but will settle for five. Anything less than five, Miranda, and you're going to have to call your husband and tell him you have to work late. Anything less is unacceptable. Understand?"

"Yes."

"See you in an hour."

The hour is plenty of time to get all of the appointments made and voice mails updated, but not near long enough to forestall the inevitable. Why do I feel like I'm on my way to the executioner's block, and why don't I just leave?

"Beau, I don't think I can do this."

"Your outfit is in the bathroom, Miranda."

Shit. Expecting the same white outfit as yesterday, minus the chastity belt, I am pleasantly surprised to see a whole new ensemble. Today it looks like Beau is going for the innocent schoolgirl look. He definitely has a thing for that virginal charm. The first piece of the outfit is a ridiculous looking white, long-sleeved, button down blouse with ruffles covering the buttons and surrounding the wrists and collar. Next is a short, plaid skirt, followed by white cotton panties, white knee socks, and black and white saddle shoes. This time, however, there is a plain white cotton bra as well, clasping in the front, nothing fancy and no padding. Set aside from the clothing are two red hair ties and a book. With a deep sigh, I begin to change.

* * *

The transformation is not nearly as devastating as yesterday's, at least not to me. Nor do I feel that same power of the irresistible temptress. Instead, I do feel more like a young woman, insecure and unsure of what to do next. Can a simple outfit mess with your head that much? Beau's voice startles me as it comes booming over the intercom in the bathroom.

"Please use the red hair ties to put your hair into two pony tails. Then grab the book and come out here. You are taking too long. I am getting restless."

I look up and around, searching for a camera or something, but can see nothing. He is either very intuitive or just damn lucky. Less than enthusiastic, I reach for the book and exit the restroom.

"You're a pervert. This isn't right."

"Excuse me?"

"I didn't know you were into little girls."

"I'm far from being 'into' little girls, Miranda. I'm into innocence, or at least the appearance of innocence, but I like the look on a hot-blooded woman like yourself. We all have our perversions. YOU just happen to be mine."

"I'm your perversion?"

"For the time being. I bought that outfit solely with you in mind, not because of a fetish for little girls."

"Oh."

"Now, if you are done insulting me, I'd like to get on with our game."

"What would you like for me to do?"

"You are going to read to me from that book. That's all."

"That's all?"

"Yes. I have every confidence nature will take its course from there. In case you haven't noticed, it's a dirty book."

Glancing down, I skim the title.

"*Sinsatiable Tales*. What's it about?"
   "It is a compilation of women's sexual fantasies."
   "I can't read this out loud to you!"
   "You can and you will. Now please have a seat in that chair directly across from my desk and begin reading to me, Miranda."

I start reading and immediately become enthralled with the first story. It's about a female prison guard getting overpowered and gang banged by several of the inmates. Not one to judge, I silently wonder about the woman who wrote down this fantasy. Halfway through the story, I begin to squirm uncomfortably.

"Getting a little warm, Miranda? Why don't you take off that blouse?"

Wishing I could make eye contact with the little pervert, I do as he requests. Soon I am sitting there in just the bra.

"How about those panties? Are they wet yet? Touch yourself. Tell me if they're wet."
   Surprised by how wet they actually are, I inform Beau, "Yes. . . . they are a little wet."
   "Just a little? We are going to have to fix that. I want you to rub your clit while you read the next few pages."

"Through my panties?"

"Yes, through your panties. Make yourself cum if you can."

Getting caught up in the story once again, I begin a tedious assault on my clit, teasing it slowly at first, and then becoming more vigorous and desperate as I near my climax. Soon it becomes too difficult to concentrate and read at the same time, so I let the book fall to the floor. My attention becomes focused completely on pleasuring myself. I throw my head back as my hips start to buck up out of the chair. With a few more magical strokes of my fingers, I reach my goal and gasp out my sweet release, feeling every clenching pulse of my pussy as it subsides. Exhausted, I look up, only to see a curtain and to hear Beau say, "Oh, baby, that was sweet. Do you like that book?"

With a slight glaze still lingering in my eyes, I nod and mumble a feeble, "Oh yeah."

"Good. Let's continue then. I want you to grab some extra cushions off of the other chair and pile them on the chair you are sitting in until you're elevated to the same height as my desk. Then scoot the chair closer until you can place the arches of your shoes on the edge of my desk with your knees bent up. Before you sit, remove your panties, but leave them resting around your ankles so your legs can only spread a short distance apart. Just pretend you're at the doctor, dear, preparing for your annual exam. Ah, I've always wondered what it would be like to be a gynecologist . . . Oh, and Miranda, be careful not to move the curtain around my desk. That would be unforgivable."

*   *   *

With the warning well understood, I begin to reposition
the chair as instructed and sit myself back down, legs
spread and feet resting on the edge of his desk.

"Raise your skirt up so that it's up around your waist.
I want to be able to see that hungry little cunt clearly."

"Do you have to be so vulgar about it?" I pout, as I
shift to get the short skirt up and out of the way.

"Yeah, I think I do. I think the nastier I talk, the more
you like it. You'd like nothing more than to be used, as
a piece of meat, over and over again, satisfying the sexual whims of anyone you came into contact with, would
you, Miranda?"

I shake my head violently from side to side, ashamed to
admit such a thing, even to myself. Am I that depraved
of a creature? But even as I deny it, I feel my blood
start to rapidly pulse and swell into the folds of my
pussy, plumping up the already glistening lips. So
quickly I find my body eager to respond to his lewd
question, my mind close behind, clouded with images of
hot, naked bodies intertwined in passionate embraces.

"Your head says, 'No,' but your body screams, 'Yes,'
Miranda. Your body was made to fuck. What a damn
shame mine wasn't. But I'm going to enjoy you just the
same, because it turns you on to perform for me, doesn't
it? Look how anxious your body is getting . . . already
rocking, your thighs flexing in and then back out again,
humping air. You want to fuck something, don't you,
baby?"

*   *   *

Unable to answer, I continue to stare at the curtain in front of me with a pained expression on my face, whimpering tiny moans of discomfort.

"Unclasp your bra and play with your tits while your body continues to fuck that imaginary cock, Miranda. You're thinking about fucking me again, aren't you?"

Gasping, I cry out, "Yes . . . ohhhh, yes! Why won't you fuck me, Beau? I release you from your promise. I don't care what you look like. Please, come fuck me . . . please. . . ."

I hear his sharp intake of breath at my pathetic plea, begging him to have his way with me. "Oh sweetheart, if only I could. You have no idea what the sight of you does to me. But I can't. Play with them."

I fumble with the front clasp of the bra in my haste to please him . . . and to provide some stimulation for my aroused body. Finally my breasts spring free and I sigh as my hands cup their exquisite softness. I begin to squeeze and caress them, pushing them close together, pulling them apart and smashing them flat to my chest as my palms glide over my distended nipples. The sensations only cause my hips to rock more insistently, while my knees and thighs attempt to touch as they flex more boldly inward.

"Pinch your nipples, baby. Pull them out toward me. Imagine me swallowing them. Imagine the suction."

Whimpering, I pinch and pull at them, shooting shards of electricity right to the center of my pussy and my throbbing clit.

*   *   *

"Oh, God, please . . . take care of me. . . ."

"Reach down between your legs and spread your lips, baby. Open wide. I want to see deep into you."

Gulping, almost panting, I snake my hands downward to delve into folds of my sex. Intense heat and wetness surround them as I gently separate the fleshy lips and pull them apart.

"Further."

Digging my fingers a little deeper into my opening, I attempt to widen myself even more.

"I can't. . . . I'm too slippery."

"Oh, yeah . . . ok, baby. You're ready for me now. Lift the right arm of the chair and take out what's hiding inside."

Reluctant to remove any stimulation from my overheated body, I lift up the arm of the chair to find a carrot, a cucumber and two clothespins guiltily waiting inside. Curiously, I notice that there are two holes drilled near the ends of the legs of the clothespins with twine threaded through. Needy for anything, I grab them all and set them on my stomach awaiting Beau's instructions.

"Put the cucumber in your mouth and suck on it. Hold it there until I tell you to take it out."

What, is he crazy? Suck on it? I'll be lucky if I can even get it to stay in my mouth. Still, I'm desperate, so

I do as he asks. Slowly my mouth widens enough to accommodate the massive intruder. Although I am unable to officially suck on it, I hold it steady with my teeth while my tongue gently licks at the tip. Satisfied that the cucumber will remain in place, Beau then tells me to take one of the clothespins and clamp it to the inner, right lip of my pussy.

"MMmrrrphhhhfff!"

"Afraid it might be painful? Oh, you'll feel it, but it won't hurt. Trust me. Then take the other clothespin and clamp it onto your inner left lip."

Hesitantly, I open the first clothespin and attach it slowly to a small section of my tender skin. There is a slight smarting initially, but within seconds it vanishes into a dull throbbing sensation, not at all unpleasant.

"No, hon. You need to get a good, meaty chunk clamped down. We're going to be pulling on those sweet lips, and we don't want those slipping off."

I re-adjust the clothespin so that it is now swallowing up a much larger section and position the other identically on the left side.

"Ah, that's more like it. Now, take the strings that are dangling down and pull them out to your sides. This will teach that naughty pussy not to open wide enough for me."

I moan in sweet torment as I begin once again to pull myself wide open for his inspection. I gasp as the cooler air rushes to mingle with my moist heat, trying to work its way inside me. Soon my pussy is resembling the mouth of a hungry baby bird, perched open to accept anything offered to it. It continues to slurp in air, mortifying me to no end with the embarrassing noises escaping it.

"Ok, baby. You can let go. Now I want you to pull your knees in toward one another. Leave your feet right where they are, but try to touch your kneecaps together."

I again do as I'm asked, desperately trying to ignore my tired jaw and the saliva beginning to seep out from the corners of my mouth.

"Keeping your knees together . . . grab the two ends of the string on the right clothespin and tie them tightly together around your right thigh. Ah . . . beautiful. Now the same with the left. Mmmmm . . . now, pull your legs apart, Miranda."

Of course, I knew what was going to happen even before I felt it. Every time I move my legs, even just a fraction, it feels like someone tugging at my pussy lips. The wider my legs fall open, the more they will be pulled and stretched. Mmmmm, it feels gloriously wicked. The rhythmic pulsing of my pelvis begins to increase in intensity, urged on by this newest form of stimulation.

"You're doing wonderfully, Miranda. It won't be long before I have you cumming all over yourself once again. Now, pick up the carrot and insert the larger end into your pussy and slowly fuck yourself with it."

Not needing any further encouragement, I pick up the carrot and examine it briefly before I lower it in place.

It's a decent size carrot, about the width of two fingers crossed together, but the intriguing part is the thicker bump about six inches down from the top running all the way around it. I can't help but wonder how that will feel as it crosses the threshold of my aching pussy. Eager to finally feel something enter me, I place the larger end of the carrot at my opening and slowly begin to penetrate it. Moaning with pleasure, I close my eyes and lay my head back while I insert it the rest of the way, gasping as I am stretched further to accommodate the extra large bump in the middle. Once the knot passes beyond, I feel my body suck up the carrot and close around it. Slowly I pull it back out, once again marveling at the added sensation the bump provides as it pauses briefly at my opening to hold me open. Soon I begin to pick up some speed, driving the carrot in and out at a faster pace. I have become even more aroused, my juicy secretions beginning to ooze freely and overflow down between my cheeks and into the cushions. I attempt to squeeze the walls of my pussy tighter, trying to grasp and pull at the carrot, but immediately become frustrated. I want more, something thicker. I want to feel full. I want the damn cucumber to replace the carrot, can't he see that? My body quickly becomes agitated and my whimpering increases.

"What's the matter, baby? Isn't that carrot big enough for you? Do you want more, Miranda?"

I begin to nod frantically, blushing at his sudden chuckling.

"Ok sweetheart. Take that juicy carrot out of your pussy and let's see you take it into your ass. I know from your earlier confessions that this is not something new to you. I want you to push it up until your ass closes over and around the nub in the middle of the carrot. Understand?"

I nod my head in acknowledgement, saliva now totally coating the cucumber and dripping down my chin and chest. I remove the carrot and begin to insert it into my ass, a bit impatient to move on to the cucumber. My ass greedily sucks it up a good six inches then pops tightly closed around the bulge, temporarily imprisoning the carrot. Only two inches are left hanging from my bottom. I begin to shiver at the sensations . . . the carrot wedged deeply into my ass, the clothespins constantly tweaking and twisting my pussy lips . . . and thoughts of where that cucumber is sure to end up. . . . My squirming increases as do the chuckles from behind the curtain.

"That cucumber looks nice and lubed up. Why don't we see how much of it you can take. You can remove it from your mouth now, but hold it right at the entrance to your pussy. Don't push it in yet."

"Oh God . . . oh God . . . oh God . . ." I manage to whisper, as I remove the massive instrument of discomfort. Oh my aching jaw . . . Gasping and slurping, I try to regain control over my mouth as I wipe myself up with the back of my hand.

"No . . . leave your face like that. I like it all wet and shiny, slick and slippery. Makes me envision something else moist and creamy adorning those sexy lips."

In no position to argue, I leave my face as is and direct my attention to the cucumber. Anxious to feel it between

---

my legs, I guide it hurriedly downward to poise waiting at the entrance to my insatiable sheath. The cucumber is huge, probably three inches thick in the center, yet this fact does not discourage me at all. Right now I am so hot and wet that I have no doubts that I'll be able to take it all.

"Hungry, puss?"

"Yes, oh, yes. Let me do it. I need to do it."

"Do what, puss?"

"Push it inside. I need to feel it inside me now."

"Go ahead, Miranda. Fuck yourself with that cucumber until you cum. Do whatever you need to do. I'm ready to watch you have another orgasm. This time, I think I'll join you."

Just as I start to slip the head of the cucumber inside, I hear the unmistakable sound of a zipper being lowered. Smiling knowingly, I return to the task at hand. Slowly I start to work the cucumber in deeper, sighing at the overwhelming feelings. I feel the pressure from the carrot, still wedged deeply in my ass, as it rubs up against the cucumber in the neighboring passage. Unable to keep still, I begin to hump wildly, pushing the cucumber further and further in . . . stretching me to my limits . . . tiny pinches reminding me of the ever present clothespins. The cucumber meets with little resistance as it becomes surrounded by generous amounts of my natural lubrication, sliding in another inch until a squeal of utmost pleasure is ripped from my throat. I begin to work it now, needing sexual release almost as much as air. I slide the cucumber back out, only to plunge it in even deeper in one, swift thrust. Again a cry escapes . . . but

I continue with the vicious assault of my own body, craving the mixture of pleasure and pain.

My other hand finds my unnaturally distended and swollen clit, probably made more apparent as the protective lips are now pulled away to the sides. It is extremely sensitive, and the first touch almost sends me over the brink. . . . but I resist, wanting this to last as long as possible. I continue to fuck myself ruthlessly with the cucumber while rubbing my clit and bouncing on the cushions, thrusting the carrot upward with each landing. Finally I can hold back no longer and buck wildly as the spasms consume me, leaving my body stiff and contorted for several seconds as the convulsions sweep through me. Before I am able to get my breathing somewhat under control, I hear several more grunts and groans followed by a long, "Aahhhhhhhhhhhhhhhhhhhhh," as Beau also reaches his own climax. Satiated, I lie back, contemplating a small nap in the overstuffed and comfy chair.

"Don't get too comfortable, doll. It's one o'clock and you've only come twice," Beau croaks out unsteadily. "You've still got some work ahead of you if you're going to make the deadline by five."

"I'm exhausted, Beau. I don't know if I can keep up this kind of pace."

"Go freshen up. When you come back, I want you completely naked."

"And you call *me* insatiable. . . ." I mutter, as I trudge off in the direction of Mr. Miller's private bathroom.

*   *   *
———

I spend ten minutes revitalizing myself, then return to the room wearing only my birthday suit.

"Ok, now what would you like for me to do?"

"Miranda . . . ah, what a lovely sight you are. How is it that you manage to look more exquisite each time I see you?"

"A curse, I can assure you."

Laughing, Beau asks me to sift through the contents of his bottom file cabinet until I've found a vibrator and a long string of anal beads.

"Take them back to the chair with you . . . and grab the book on the way. I think it's time for more reading."

I settle myself back into the chair in much the same position as before, only this time my ankles are not restricted by the panties, and I can part my legs as wide as I like. They are still bent, and my feet are still resting on the edges of his desk, but I have since done away with the carrot, cucumber and clothespins.

"Before you start reading, I want you to insert those anal beads. There should be eight of them attached together on that string. That should be enough to keep you feeling pleasantly full."

Totally without inhibitions and reservations, I spread my legs wide and begin to press the anal beads into my ass as if it were the most natural thing in the world for me to be doing. Although I have cooled down a bit, I am still overstimulated and looking forward to giving Beau a show. Again my ass becomes a creature all its own and sucks in each and every last bead offered to it, pouting when they have all been eaten.

"God, Miranda. Your ass loves to be fucked just as much as your pussy does."

Sighing, I squirm down into the cushions, relishing the feeling as the beads shift and move around inside me. Finally settled, I begin to read another erotic story. Within a half of an hour, I am once again aroused and looking forward to another orgasm. This time Beau has me turn on the vibrator and use it only on my clit, not allowing it to penetrate me. I continue to read as sweat begins to bead up on my forehead from the constant vibrations coursing through my body at my clit. When I can no longer concentrate on the words I am reading, I cast the book aside and begin to remove the anal beads while the vibrator continues to happily buzz along my clit. As the last bead is removed, my body is thrown into its third orgasm of the day, this time visibly squirting liquid outward with each separate convulsion.

"Oh my God, Beau . . . that's never happened before . . . I've never . . . ejaculated before . . . I . . . I'm. . . . Oh, God . . ."

"Oh baby! I've never seen a woman do that before, either! What an incredible turn on! I'm never going to be able to let you go . . . "

Gasping, I try to relax back into the cushions, watching and feeling the goosebumps slowly recede, amazed that even my scalp came to life and tingled throughout that last orgasm. "Beau, I can't do this anymore. My body is worn out."

"Miranda, there's nothing that turns me on more than a challenge. It's going to be all the sweeter when you do cum for me again knowing that you thought you had reached your limit. I want to enter your mind and control your body, bending and shaping it, molding and manipulating it. I want it to react to me and for me . . . and then I want to do it all over again."

"Beau . . . "

By five o'clock, as promised, Beau manages to extract from me yet another orgasm, relying solely on his own verbal skills and my practiced hands. For two hours he speaks dirty to me, invoking raw and primal images, carrying me to places I had yet to discover, drawing from me even more of my darkest thoughts. I am utterly spent, but still he is not satisfied, and won't be until I've shared my fifth and final orgasm with him. Reluctantly, I stumble out to my own desk to call the house and inform Nick that I will have to work late this lovely Friday night.

"Hello."

"Hi, hon. I have some bad news. I'm going to have to work late tonight. Mr. Miller needs my help getting some deadlines met. I'm sorry."

"No problem, Randa. I'll probably just head down to the pub for a couple of drinks. If I'm not home when you get home, look for me there."

"Okay, great. I'll be ready to have a few myself. It's already been a really long day."

"Tell me all about it when you get here, okay? I love ya."

"I love you too. See you soon."

The fifth orgasm is by far the most elusive, but by 9:30 PM, Beau is whistling victoriously, and I am vowing to never again touch myself for self-gratification. I agree to return to work Monday morning only after he promises me that the activities of today will never again be repeated. Exhausted, I exit the building, immediately perking up as I discover the beauty of the night. It is warm, yet refreshing, the air very fragrant with nature's finest scents, reminding me of why I moved to the small mountain community in the first place. Revitalized, I continue my short trek home.

CHAPTER 6

■

EXPLOITATIONS

I am disappointed to learn that Nick is not at home when I get there, but that quickly dissipates as I read the rather intriguing note left behind. Typed in all capital letters, it simply reads: MEET ME AT THE BASE-BALL DIAMOND.

Now what is he up to, I wonder with a large grin, another game perhaps? That's one we hadn't discussed before. . . . the baseball player and the ???? I can't even imagine what my role is supposed to be. Hmmm, maybe I am supposed to be the baseball player and he the ????? Excitedly, I hurry and freshen up, changing into a comfy pair of jeans, a long-sleeved T-shirt and a pair of tennies. Then, racing out the door, I head in the direction of the baseball diamond.

The ball field is located just a short walk from my house, actually on the local high school's property. It is situated way toward the back of the school, beyond the track in a very dark and secluded section. During the daytime, the location seems innocent enough, but at night, without any lighting to humble it, it seems dark and foreboding. Nick must have known that I would get a charge out of meeting him in such a creepy place. Immediately, my sexually fatigued body begins to awaken in anticipation for the unknown delights that Nick has in store for me.

The baseball diamond appears to be deserted when I arrive. No sign of any activity at all making it seem even more sinister.

"Nick?" I whisper. "Are you here? Yoo hoo, Nick?"
  Immediately, a hand comes from behind me to cover my mouth, and a soft, "shhhhh" is whispered into my ear. I overcome my momentary panic and elect to play along as Nick guides me to the chain-link fence backstop. The backstop is about ten feet high and shaped like half of a hexagon. He walks me over to the far right of the fence and pushes me up against it whispering another "shhhhh" as he removes his hand from my mouth. He keeps one hand pressed into the back of my head, not allowing me to turn my face to look at him.

"Nick? What are you doing?"

Again, all I hear is another, "shhhhhh" accompanied by a blindfold being placed over my eyes. I shudder, despite the warm night. Confident that I cannot see, Nick turns me around so that my back is pressed flat up against the backstop, the metal chain somewhat uncomfortable. The next thing I feel is something soft and silky being draped around my neck and through the chain of the fence. My God . . . he's tying me to the fence by my neck! I feel him move around to the backside of the fence to complete the process, making sure I can go nowhere without strangling myself.

One simple maneuver. One simple knot, yet the havoc that it is creating in my mind is boundless. Immobilized by one tiny silk scarf! Unbelievable. The pressure against my throat, enough to remind me it's there, but not enough to choke me, not unless I struggle. Even with my hands free, it would take hours to maneuver my fingers successfully to untie the knot fastening me to the fence. Next, Nick takes my right arm and draws it out to the side, slightly lower than my shoulder with the inside of my wrist positioned down and against the fence. Subconsciously, my fingers reach out and grip a section of the chain as I feel another scarf binding my wrist to it. Nick does the same with my left arm and wrist, tethering me to the backstop completely with three gentle scarves.

"Nick . . . what if somebody walks by? Or worse . . . uh, sorry, officer. We're just trying to spice up our sex life a bit."

For an answer, Nick presses his body flat against mine. I can hear his deeply impassioned breathing, smell the slight odor of alcohol with each puff of air expelled. And then the kiss. . . . oh, so completely consuming, rocking me to my toes. A kiss that says, "You belong to me . . . you are mine . . . I own you body and soul." A desperate kiss . . . a hungry kiss . . . His hands stroke my body as he continues his onslaught, his chest rubbing into and across mine. His mouth leaves my lips to gently nip at the skin on my face, my cheeks, my chin, and then down my throat. I begin to moan, knowing that it is Nick's intent to take me . . . right there, against the backstop. Granted, the probability of getting discovered isn't great, but it still exists.

"Nick . . . Nick . . ." I gasp out between delicious waves of pleasure, "We can't do this here. Somebody is bound to catch us."

Again, Nick says nothing, but the kissing and grinding stop. I wait nervously, breathlessly, wondering what his next move is going to be. Did he finally come to his senses and realize that this was too risky? No such luck, I come to find out, as I feel the cool edge of steel placed against my slightly parted lips. A knife?!? What the hell is he using a knife for? I begin to shake in panic, afraid to even speak lest the blade accidentally pierce my lip. Instead, I whimper and subconsciously press my body deeper into the chain-link fence.

The blade leaves my lips and begins a slow, tickling descent, down my chin, down my throat, grazing the silk scarf before it stops to tease the hollow of my neck. I try desperately to reason with my fear, to calm myself knowing that Nick would never hurt me. It's a game. He's trying to help me live out that "rape" fantasy . . . that has to be it, and he's just making it as realistic as possible. The fact that I'm still blindfolded proves it. If I could see him, make eye contact with him, none of these feelings would be the same. I'd automatically feel safe and secure no matter what device of torture he held in front of me.

I suck in my breath as the knife leaves my throat, and I feel his other hand tug at my shirt. Unable to keep my knees from shaking, I try to stand perfectly still as my shirt is untucked from my jeans. Then I hear a soft tearing sound as the blade is inserted through the bottom of my shirt and begins to slowly travel upward. Terror consumes me as the knife begins to split my shirt in half, the warm night air rushing in to meet my belly, yet even as I cringe, my body begins to respond sexually. It has been awakened on a whole different level, by far the darkest yet. This supercedes any bondage game that Nick and I have played in the past. This is for real, and it's scaring the hell out of me. But it's also the most powerful aphrodisiac to date, arousing me more quickly and to new heights than I ever thought possible. Every nerve ending is awakened, every sense intensified, every breath magnified, every shudder electric. My body is being held in such a state that it is precariously close to short circuiting. A sharp cry is emitted as the blade slices through the final shred of cloth at my collarbone, and then dips back down to cut away the tiny patch of satin holding my bra together.

"Oh, God . . ." I groan as my breasts spring free, my knees collapsing, only momentarily as a painful tug reminds me that the scarf at my throat is not quite enough to hold my weight. Grasping the fence, I quickly call on the strength in my arms to help steady my shaking limbs. Mewling, I sigh in disguised rapture as I feel soft, wet, warm lips make contact with my already responsive nipple. The mouth stays there, suckling gently, licking, feasting, concentrating on nothing else. No hands accompany it . . . just a mouth, an endless cavern of bliss. Each time my nipple is sucked in more deeply, another pulse of pleasure beats violently in my throbbing clit. Before I am even aware that it is happening myself, my body jerks forcefully as another orgasm seizes control of my muscles and sends catastrophic waves of exhilaration throughout my being, from the top of my head to the tips of my toes.

Nick doesn't let it stop there, but changes nipples and begins to suck more vigorously while rubbing at my clit and pussy through my jeans. Not only does my orgasm *not* subside, but it continues to build, the spasms and pulses becoming greater and more intense, releasing, throbbing, building, then releasing again. Over and over I peak then crash, only to immediately peak again. Unable to contain myself, I begin to scream out, only to have the sound cut off as Nick entombs my mouth with his own, swallowing any evidence of my audible elation and imprisoning it within the pit of his belly. When the last wave of ecstasy finally recedes, Nick is forced to hold me upright, certain that I'll choke to death if left to my own devices.

Tiny kisses on the top of my head are the first sensations to greet me as I begin to recover. As more of my senses become functional again, I realize that I had just had the most mind-blowing orgasm of the century, multiple orgasms at that.

"Oh my God, Nick. That was too unbelievable for words."

* * *

My hips and ass begin to gyrate backward into the fence as I relive the incredible encounter I just went through. And even though I am completely satiated, I want more. My pussy is begging to be filled. All that stimulation, all that pleasure, yet none of it directly involved the heart of my womanhood.

"Oh, Nick . . . I need to feel you inside me, right now. Complete me, please."

Instead of feeling his fingers on the buttons of my jeans, I feel them working on removing my blindfold. I guess now that the initial game of fear is over, it is okay to see him as he takes me on the remainder of this monumental journey. I want it hot, I want it rough, I want it frenzied . . . and I want it now. Urgently. As soon as my blindfold is removed, I gaze into Nick's sky blue eyes . . . wait . . . oh God . . . Nick's eyes are brown . . .

My bloodcurdling scream is immediately stifled by Russ's large hand.

"Jesus Christ, Miranda. You don't need to scream. I haven't hurt you, and I don't intend to. Re-fucking-lax!"

I am speechless for several minutes as my mind absorbs the implications of what I've just discovered. Russ! It can't be . . . it couldn't have been . . . Oh God . . . it was . . . Russ? Russ is responsible for all that glorious bliss I just experienced? Russ? Evil, perverted, scary Russ? It's not possible, but here he is, standing in front of me as cocky and proud as always. The son of a bitch! In this moment, I can't decide if I'm more scared, or pissed. . . . or . . . horny. Oh God.

*   *   *

Russ removes his hand from my mouth hesitantly, prepared to slam it back over if another peep should escape. My mouth remains poised open in a witless "O," but silent. He watches the confused expressions cross my face with amusement, then ventures, "Still want me to fuck you, Mirandaaaahhhhhh?"

"What have you done with Nick?"

"Nick's fine. I took him out drinking. He's sleeping it off in the comfort of his very own bed. Promise . . ."

"How did you know?"

"How did I know what, sweetums? How did I know you were going to have to work late tonight? I can just imagine what you were doing, too. I bet your cunt is dripping with Mr. Miller's semen right now, isn't it? You stayed late so you could boff the boss . . ."

"I did no such thing!" I reply, indignantly. . . . then calm myself as I remember exactly why I did stay late. An embarrassed flush spreads accusingly across my face.

"Yeah, I thought so. Nick called and invited me out for drinks to pass the time. He played right into my hands. I think he wanted to talk to me about not sending you any more e-mails, but he got a little sidetracked. It was perfect timing, and so easy."

"What are you going to do with me?"

"Are you a little scared, Miranda? Of little ole me?"

"Russ, quit toying with me! You win, you've got me. I just want to know what you plan to do with me."

"Oh, listen to the martyr. Just five minutes ago you were begging me to fuck your brains out. I know what seethes below the surface, Miranda, and I know how to awaken it."

"Russ . . . "

"I'm prepared to let you go right now. But I bet . . . if you dig deep . . . you'll discover that you don't want me to let you go. You want to ride this out and see what happens, don't you? Admit it, Miranda. The thought of what awaits you in my dungeon excites you. Nobody else can make you feel like this, Miranda, not even Nick. I promise to deliver you unharmed to your husband first thing Monday morning, but for the weekend you'll be totally and completely at my mercy. What do you say, Miranda? Shall I continue with the complete ravishment of your body?"

Oh heaven help me. . . . the fact that I'm even considering it proves that I need psychological counseling. I say nothing as tears well up in my eyes and my body breaks out into a cold sweat.

"Miranda. . . . you're thinking about it, aren't you? You want this to happen so badly, yet you can't give your consent. I need a, 'yes,' baby. I've never taken a woman against her will, and I'm not going to start now. But I would love to rape you, with your permission, of course. Give it to me. . . . say, 'yes.' "

"Russ . . . you're insane. I can't say yes to this."

"Yes you can. You want to, I can feel it. It's easy. Just say yes. One little word."

Russ reaches a hand to my face and squishes my lips and cheeks inward, making my mouth pucker up like a blowfish.

"Yyyyyyyes," he says again, mouthing the word while squeezing my lips. "Yes, Russ. I'd like nothing more than for you to have your way with me all weekend. Do it Russ. Come on Miranda. It's right there on the tip of your tongue. Let me help get it for you."

Russ again captures my lips with his own, extracting from them my resistance, making me respond to his kiss, and not to Nick's. Grabbing my tongue between his teeth, he begins to suck on it, pulling it into his own mouth, teasing it with his own tongue. He continues to toy with it, plundering my mouth, his tongue slithering down my throat, drawing the breath from my lungs, then moving deeper. I feel him in my gut, twisting lower, not satisfied until he tugs at my sex from the inside, gripping it, squeezing it, making it burn from a hunger left too long unfed. Gasping in resignation, I finally utter the word he wants to hear.

"Mmmonkey."

Releasing my lips, he gazes back at me. "Monkey? Close, but not quite." He continues to grin maliciously, knowing full well the word I had so painfully spoken.

"I said . . . okay. Okay, Okay, Okay!"

"My, my, my. Now we're a little over anxious, aren't we? Okay, what, baby doll?"

"Damn it, Russ! Don't mess with me . . . I'll take it back . . ."

Russ begins to stroke his finger lightly up and down my throat as if placating an angry kitten.

"Shhhhh . . . okay, what, baby doll?"

Ohhhhh . . . SEX . . . is absolutely dripping from his voice. What am I doing?

*　　*　　*

"O. . . . kay . . . I'll go with you for the weekend," I stammer out, feeling suddenly drugged.

"Nooooo. . . . I want to hear, 'Okay, Russ . . . yes, Russ . . . I want you to rape me. . . . I want you to use my body . . . I want you to take me to the depths of hell and then to the pinnacle of pleasure, all in the same moment. Yes, Russ.' "

"Yes . . . Russ . . ." I gasp . . .

"I give you permission . . . "

"I give you permission . . . " Oh, God . . . I can't believe I'm saying this . . .

"To use and abuse my body. . . ."

"To use and abuse my body. . . ." Whimpering. . . .

"I want you to rape me. . . ."

"Uhhhhhh . . . rape . . . me . . . "

Russ growls and in a matter of moments, he's possessed. Something gets shoved inside my mouth . . . another scarf, maybe . . . and then another is placed over my mouth and tied around my head and through the chain-link of the backstop, holding my head as still as my neck. With this aggressive turn of events, my natural instinct to fight takes over, and I begin to kick out at Russ, my legs being my only body part left free. He curses and shoves his knee into my crotch, then throws his entire body weight against me. Then he whispers dangerously into my ear, "God damn it, Miranda. I'm going to have you one way or the other. If you want there to be bruises, then keep fighting me. And . . . don't forget. . . . about my little friend here, Mr. Switchblade."

My eyes widen in surprise and terror as I come face to face with the knife I had felt earlier. It is ten times more menacing than anything my mind had envisioned, and I immediately cease my struggles.

"That's better."

He closes the switchblade and then places it in his shirt pocket. Pressed nose to nose, he begins to fumble with the buttons on my jeans.

"You smell like sex, Miranda. It's seeping from your pores."

Don't panic, don't panic, don't panic. He's not going to hurt me. I asked him to do this. Oh, God. . . . I'm even getting wet. Soaked. I'm soaked, I can feel the fluids gushing from my center. Oh, God, hurry. Get it over with. Please.

Soon he has my jeans unbuttoned and begins to yank them downward, taking my panties with them. Stopping at mid-thigh, his hand immediately reaches for my exposed pussy and grasps at it roughly. He never takes his eyes from mine, thriving on my reactions, my eyes revealing every thought, every feeling. He begins to work his fingers inside . . . two of them? Three? Oh. . . . could it be four? I feel them curl and then pull back out again, removing with them large amounts of my intimate juices. He brings his hand to his nose and takes a big sniff . . . closing his eyes in delight as he does so.

"Hmmmm . . . maybe you weren't fucking Mr. Miller after all. There's nothing here but sweet Miranda. Smell for yourself."

* * *

He shoves his fingers into my nose, and then begins to rub them all around it, leaving me with a permanent reminder of how hot and wanton I truly smell. The remainder of my flavor is sucked off of his sticky fingers as he eagerly inserts them into his greedy mouth.

"Oh yeah, oh yeah, oh . . . yeah. . . . ," Russ mutters between noisy slurps. "Time to lose the jeans."

Pushing himself off of me, he bends down and busies himself with the task of removing my shoes and then my jeans and panties. I assist him in every way possible, concerned that he may get frustrated and bring Mr. Switchblade back into the picture to cut them away . . . and then some. All goes smoothly enough, and I breathe a sigh of relief. A short-lived sigh, however, as my legs are immediately pulled out from under me to be cradled in the crooks of his arms. Then without any warning, I am skewered, impaled on his rock-hard cock to the hilt. If I could scream, I would, the shock so overwhelming. But not from pain. . . . Oh help me, but it's deliriously wonderful. Exceptional. Savagely, he thrusts into me, pulling my body away from the backstop, just far enough for me to feel the tug at my throat, and then slamming me back into it. Over and over he continues with the vicious assault, my body gladly taking it and then asking for more. Time stands still. Nothing exists but his cock relentlessly plunging into the depths of my sex . . . ruthless . . . sadistic. My body knows none of this, basking instead in the frenzied excitement, welcoming each brutal thrust with open arms. Finally he collapses against me in a fit of convulsions. . . . the first in a series of how many?

Stepping back, Russ studies me silently as he regains his balance.

"You liked that, didn't you? Miranda, you're a woman after my own heart. I'll bet you can keep up with me, kinky stroke for kinky stroke. I guess I'll find out this weekend, won't I?"

Unable to answer, I continue to stare at him, shivers returning. He stoops down to pull up his own jeans, which have managed to worm their way down to his ankles during the physical onslaught. Now that my initial encounter with Russ is over, I can release some of the fear I had been harboring over the last several months. All those threatening poems had been sending my imagination into overdrive. I'm not sure what I had expected would happen if Russ ever did manage to follow through with his plans, but intensely thrilling, wild sex was not one of them. Am I actually looking forward to being taken to his torture chamber?

I examine Russ more closely as he gathers up my things . . . my shoes, my jeans, and then begins to walk away into the trees behind the backstop. A momentary panic envelops me as I imagine him leaving me here this way, but the feeling soon passes. I gave him a weekend. He wouldn't pass that up, would he? Well, I could be in worse positions. At least I now know that Russ isn't going to hurt me. That's a huge relief. And, well, if you're going to be used and abused by someone for a weekend, it might as well be someone like Russ. Anyone that asks for your permission before he rapes you has to have some shred of a conscience, and . . . well, as much as I hate to admit it, he is definitely easy to look at. The contrast between those sky blue eyes and that jet black hair is pretty spectacular. He also has the physique of a body builder, only taller, and has managed to maintain his neck in the process. I attempt to shake my head in exasperation at the insanity of my thoughts, but the scarves still bind me tightly.

"What is going on in that pretty head of yours? Your eyes are going a hundred miles an hour. Were you worried there for a minute that I was going to leave you?" Russ taunts.

Asshole. My eyes narrow into slits. Russ walks back over to me, close enough that I can feel his body heat, smell his breath. He reaches into his shirt pocket with an evil smile on his face and withdraws the switchblade, holding it directly in front of my eyes. The blade pops up without warning, startling me to the point of tears, my heart plummeting to my stomach for immediate digestion. I close my eyes, a feeble attempt at reducing the menacing threat that the blade signifies. Russ only chuckles, and moves to the back side of the fence, cutting through the delicate silk ties imprisoning my face and neck. Russ removes the scarves and tucks them into his pants pocket while returning to the front to check on his progress. As soon as I am able, I spit out the wad in my mouth, hitting him square in the chest.

"An act of defiance, Miranda? Good. It'll make it all the more fun when I break you."

Another malicious grin. I look down in time to see the knife being slowly slipped between the back of my right wrist and the silk scarf securing it there. Russ makes a dramatic display, keeping me on edge far longer than is necessary, then boldly slices through it. Ah, at last my arm is free. I immediately pull it away and begin to shake it. Before Russ frees my other arm, however, my right wrist is greeted with the cold, clinking metal of a handcuff.

"I'm not going to make this too easy on you. I don't want you getting away."

"I promised to go with you, Russ, and I will. You don't need to handcuff me."

"Maybe not, but let's pretend I do . . . "

Rolling my eyes, I stand stoically by while Russ cuts the other arm away from the fence and then pulls both arms behind my back and cuffs them together. Russ then grabs the tops of my legs and lifts me up and over his shoulder, forcing all the air from my lungs. He quickly starts walking back into the trees and dumps me into the back seat of his awaiting Jeep. The vinyl is chilling as it makes contact with my bare ass, reminding me of how naked I am. Although I have what's left of my shirt still on, it is sliced clean up the front with my bra pushed around and to the back, and nothing below my waist except for my little white ankle socks. The ride to Russ's house is brutal, unable to ascertain which emotion is more prevalent . . . dread . . . or anticipation.

"Welcome to the dungeon, my little house of horrors, where you will be spending the remainder of the weekend."

* * *

I wander in with trepidation, gulping at sights I had only previously seen in pictures, and some I had never seen, or even heard of before. The room is square with mirrors covering all four walls from floor to ceiling. Half of the room looks clinical; white, tile, ceramic, tables, counters . . . and a huge floor drain right in the middle. The other half of the room is dark and wooden . . . wooden padded benches and a huge, free-standing wooden wheel that looks like something right out of a giant gerbil's cage. I glance around warily to assure myself that no oversized rodent lurked nearby. There are several ladders, most suspended from the ceiling, ropes, pulleys, and a wooden and glass display case flaunting an extensive array of whips and paddles.

Russ leads me around, gently guiding me by the elbow, as if giving a grand tour to the Queen of England herself. First he explains the devices and some of their uses found in the white section of the room. There is a counter similar to what you would see in a doctor's office, with a built-in sink and a carton of disposable rubber gloves sitting off to the side. Above the counter is a cabinet with glass doors, making the contents inside quite visible. There are several jars containing a wide variety of herbs, as well as creams, lotions and lubricants. Stupefied, I continue with the tour.

In the far back corner is the shower/bath area. The huge jacuzzi tub sits innocently enough against the far left mirrored wall. Facing the adjacent mirrored wall is what Russ refers to as his seesaw ladder. It looks just like a seesaw only shorter, wider, and in the shape of a ladder with rungs only located on the top third section.

All the rungs and sides of the ladder are made from white padded vinyl, and at the very top, closest to the mirrored wall, is a headrest like you'd find on a massage table. Russ is able to stabilize the seesawing action by a lever, permitting the ladder to be secured at any angle. The ladder is also built on a hydraulic base and can be raised and lowered to any height that Russ desires.

The next piece of furniture that Russ discusses at length is a white table with rounded edges and sides standing a little higher than waist high. On top of the table is a white stockade, with a hole cut out for the head, and two smaller holes for the wrists. It doesn't raise up very high off the table, and Russ explains that the women are usually kneeling on the table while enjoying the stockade, facing outward toward the "wooden" half of the room, her bottom facing the jacuzzi tub.

Directly across from the seesaw ladder, is nothing other than a doctor's table, complete with stirrups. The back of the table adjusts so that you can either be lying flat on it, or sitting up completely straight. I imagine this position would be somewhat uncomfortable if your feet were in the stirrups at the same time . . . shudder.

Next Russ takes me over into the wooden half of the room, allowing only some of my curiosities about the huge wheel to be appeased. Russ has me step inside it as I make my inspection. There is enough room inside for someone at least six and a half feet tall to stand upright. The depth of the wheel is probably only two feet deep, with four inch wide wooden slats spaced a half an inch apart running all along the inside of the wheel. The interior is very sturdy, quite capable of holding my weight several times over. I ask Russ what the wheel is used for, but he just grins and tells me that I'll find out soon enough.

There are also a few spanking benches scattered throughout the room, a swing similar to my virtual reality swing, only not . . . a thick beam off to the side running from ceiling to floor with a narrow metal bar protruding from it about twelve inches, and another wooden stockade, only this one taller and standing on the floor. The last thing he shows me is the bondage bed, which is pretty much a glorified air mattress, all in black, with extra reinforcements to house the clips, clamps and eyelets running along all four sides.

Russ looks over at me again as if trying to decide where to start. Unwittingly, I make his decision for him.

"Russ. I need to use the bathroom."
    "Certainly. But let's get you out of these rags, first."

Thinking this isn't going to be so bad, I relax as Russ undoes the handcuffs and then removes the rest of my clothing, socks included. When I am completely naked, Russ replaces the handcuffs and whistles appreciatively.

"Ah, yes, that's the body I remember so well from the poker game."

Why did he have to mention the poker game? I watch his features closely, wondering if those memories are going to make him angry, but they don't appear to. Relieved, I follow Russ back on over into the white room. He has me stand on the drain and then moves to get his rolling white stool and sits down watching me.

"What are you doing?"

"You said you needed to use the bathroom. There it is."

"This drain?" I ask incredulous. "You want me to relieve myself in this drain?"

"Yup." He says, with a nasty smile.

"While you watch?"

"Yup again. You don't mind, do you?" He asks as innocently as possible.

"Of course I mind, Russ. I can't go with you watching me."

"Well, you'd better get used to it, because what you see is what you get. I doubt you can hold it all weekend. Besides, this is just a mild humiliation. I've got more in store for you."

A cold feeling of trepidation begins seep through me. I had forgotten what this was all about. This isn't a game, and it's certainly not going to be played by my rules. I gave myself to Russ . . . to use, to abuse . . . to even rape. What the hell was I thinking? And this is Russ we are talking about. He is by far the most sexually deviant person I've even known, myself included.

"What if I change my mind? What if I no longer want to spend the weekend with you. You said you've never forced a woman before and never would."

*　　*　　*

Russ looks me over thoughtfully. "You've obviously already forgotten the excitement of the backstop, haven't you? I can turn your insides to mush with just a look, Miranda. You won't change your mind. You can't change your mind. You need this. Look at me."

I glance up and immediately get ensnared by the intensity of his eyes. They are hypnotic, and I am helpless to deny them.

"Now piss."

I remain frozen, rooted to the spot, unable to respond. Russ bends over and takes off his shoes and socks, then stands up and begins to remove the rest of his clothing. His captive gaze never wavers from mine as his shirt disappears, and then his pants. Within moments, he is standing as naked as I, challenging me to disobey him.

"Piss."

Still, I cannot move, my brain ceasing to function. This is the first time I have seen Russ completely without clothing, and he's quite the specimen. Perfect symmetry, a sculpture come to life. Even as he stalks purposefully toward me, I am unable to flee or even look away. He presses his naked body into mine and pulls my head backward by my hair.

"I said piss, Miranda. We're going to stay like this until you do."

Russ then lowers his head and begins to kiss me. Oh, God . . . how can he kiss like this? Sweet, tender, yearning, begging, pleading, coaxing . . . magical. His kisses are magical, and he knows it and uses them to manipulate. Right now he could be threatening me with a beating, forcing me with brute strength, yet his strategy is to softly but slowly wear me down, kissing away any shred of resistance. It worked at the ball field, and it's working now.

I feel his other hand dip down to nestle between my legs, gently fondling the folds of my pussy. He pulls his mouth away from mine occasionally to whisper words of encouragement, then immediately returns it to the task of seducing my heated lips.

"Come on baby . . . Piss on my hand . . . Just let it go. . . . Let yourself go . . ."

I whimper, torn between saving my modesty and succumbing to his wishes. I feel a long, strong finger enter me, and I swoon at the welcome invasion. Russ slowly and leisurely explores my volcanic interior, while his thumb absently rubs at my clit.

"Piss for me baby. I'm going to find your G-spot in a second, and then you won't be able to stop yourself."

Why do these words suddenly sound sexy to me? Is it the heated way in which he is mumbling them, against my mouth, my nose and my chin as he kisses me? And why do I have this unexpected urge to please him? It would be so easy . . . just to let go . . . and fill his waiting palm. Just as my decision is reached, Russ's knowing finger finds and puts pressure against my G-spot, massaging it slowly yet persistently. His thumb continues to work on my clit, the dual assault more than I can handle. In an instant, he has me convulsing in orgasm as I simultaneously release myself into his hand. Damn him, damn him, damn him! I feel his mouth stretch into a smile as he finally pulls away and breaks the compelling and persuasive kiss.

"That wasn't so bad, was it?" he asks, as he moves to grasp the retractable faucet built into the pedestal of the gyno table. Turning on the water, he rinses off his hand and then directs the spray toward the drain, washing away any evidence of my recent disgrace.

"Before this night is over, toots, I'm going to become very intimate with each and every one of your bodily functions. Now, you've got ten seconds to get that sweet ass of yours up onto that gyno table."

Wrought with apprehension, I jump up onto the table and face him. He adjusts his stool height so that he is pretty much eye level with my navel. Then he adjusts the back of the padded table so that it is resting at an approximate 45-degree angle. Next, one cuff is removed as I am gently coaxed backwards until reclining comfortably against it. Never would I have assumed that a torture chamber could be so cozy, and its master so gentle. Before long I feel my arms being pulled back and around the edges of the angled table to be once again cuffed behind it.

"Feet in the stirrups, baby."

* * *

Cringing, I resist. I don't want to be that open and vulnerable to anyone, let alone Russ. Shaking his head in mock disappointment, Russ pulls my legs up one at a time and places each foot into a stirrup, securing them there with vinyl straps. Testing them, I attempt to remove my feet, but they remain firmly locked in place. Unable to bear witness to this newest form of humiliation, I squeeze my eyes shut and refuse to even glance at Russ.

Russ, on the other hand, is unconcerned and walks on over toward the sink area, washing his hands thoroughly. I hear him digging through the cupboard above, and then whistle while preparing the next surprise he has in store for me. I risk a quick peek in his direction, my curiosity always getting the best of me, but am thwarted from seeing anything other than his broad back and shoulders. Again, I find my imagination my own worst enemy as I try to conceive what form of torture he's certain to use on my very exposed and very defenseless pussy.

Russ returns gently shaking a very familiar looking pink bag.

"I'm going to clean you up, inside and out, before I get you all messy again," he declares with a smile.

"What did you mix inside?" I ask, accepting my fate passively.

Grinning, he reveals, "Ah, only my most potent and special herbs. I'm going to make sure that I awaken your pretty pussy and that she's going to want to play all night long."

"I can't believe this! You're drugging me?"

"Drugging is such a harsh term, Miranda. It's more like I'm applying a topical . . . itch. An itch that's impossible to scratch, although we'll have fun trying."

"Russ, don't, please. I'm cooperating, just like I said I would."

"Forgive me if your submissive martyrdom isn't exactly what I was hoping for. This is guaranteed to unleash the wild beast I know you hide within. Here kitty, kitty. Come out and play. . . ."

Russ reaches up and yanks on a pulley, hanging the douche bag to it, then releasing it back upward. Then he sets the end of the hose and nozzle to rest in the crease of my leg.

"Hmmmm . . . let's see. You look too plain. We need to fancy you up a bit."

He leaves me momentarily, only to return with a stunning white rhinestone collar and two nipple clamps. The clamps have a pearl necklace draped between them, and a heavy looking crystal hanging down from each one. Russ cinches the collar around my neck without any fuss, but as soon as he approaches a nipple with a clamp, I begin to struggle and squirm.

"Russ . . . Russ . . . please . . . I've never worn that type of clamp before, and never with any weight to them. Do you have a different pair?"

Russ looks up in amazement. "Miranda, when are you going to learn that you are not running this show? These are the clamps you will wear, and by Sunday night, you'll have three crystals dangling from each, instead of only one."

I hold my breath, waiting for the excruciating pinch, only to feel his soft lips begin to gently suckle at my nipple. I sigh in relief and yield to the pleasant sensations as Russ begins to increase the sucking pressure. Soon I am moaning and yelping as the gentle suction has turned to pulling and biting, working my nipple and preparing it for the clamp. I screech as his mouth is removed and the clamp takes its place, trapping all of that blood into my distended nipple. Immediately, a surge of moisture floods my gaping pussy. Russ does the same with my other nipple and then takes his place between my outspread thighs. I rock my head back and forth moaning, alternating between hating the feel of those clamps and loving it.

Russ quickly gets my attention diverted back to him as I feel the stirrups slowly clicking their way outward. Horrified, I find my thighs, knees, calves and ankles widening with each clicking sound until they are held at an obscenely uncomfortable distance apart. Russ is gleeful as he lowers his head into my widely displayed crotch and begins to lick.

"My, my. You've already made quite the mess down here, haven't you? Are you enjoying this? Do you love being my little captive, at the mercy of my every whim?"

I only whimper in response, confused between the mortification I feel and the delicious sensations shooting through my nipples and now . . . my throbbing clit. Russ makes an exaggerated sniffing sound then buries his nose into my opening.

"Mirandaaaa. . . . I can still smell my fuck in you . . ."

I cry out . . . my shame increasing with each passing moment. Russ lifts his face from my crotch and takes the end of the hose, still nestled in the crook of my leg. Grinning lewdly, he slowly begins to insert the nozzle, while my traitorous hips instinctually rock forward to greet it. Then he releases the clamp, and I begin to feel the warm liquid penetrate and coat me. Russ moves the nozzle all around, making sure the herbs make contact with every inch of my satiny interior. Before too long, the bag is half empty and liquid begins to dribble out and down the table.

The herbs are already taking affect as I feel my insides pulsing with need. With each passing minute, the twitching increases, and my clit answers back with its own desperate throbbing. Russ empties the bag and then removes the nozzle, allowing the remainder of the douche to dribble out at will.

"Russ . . . oh God . . . Oh God, Russ. . . ."

"Ah, starting to feel it, aren't you? And it's going to get much, much worse before it gets better, hon."

"Fuck me . . ." I whisper, barely audible.

"Excuse me? I missed that, Miranda. Say it again."

Gritting my teeth, I force out, "I said. . . . Fuck me!"

"Hmmmm, you're not asking very nicely at all. Where are your manners?"

"God damn it, Russ . . . you know . . . what . . . this is. . . . doing to me. Please. . . . please help me."

"Oh . . . is Miranda uncomfortable? This is how my dick and my balls have ached for you every day since the poker game. I've felt this torture for nine months. Feel lucky you'll only feel it for two days."

"Russ . . . please, Russ. I'm sorry . . . it was . . . Nick . . . Nick's idea . . . in the first place. I . . . didn't know . . . you . . . didn't know . . . how. . . . it would . . . affect you. Ssssorry. . . . so sorry, Russ."

The herbs are setting me on fire, so intense I can barely breathe. I want to be fucked. I want to be fucked and fucked and fucked. Russ stands, wanting to punish me by only watching as my desire mounts, yet unable to deny himself the erotic delights on display as I continue to squirm and beg. Soon he gives into his own impulses and drives his imposing erection deep into the fury of my heat. Gripping my thighs for balance, he begins to plunge into me. With each punishing thrust, more water and herbs are pumped from me, the herbs certain to affect his libido as well. As if possessed, I begin to urge him on.

"Oh yeah . . . oh yeah . . . oh yeah. . . . Fuck me, Russ. Yes . . . deeper . . . oh God yes . . . harder . . . come on . . . fuck me harder. . . . Ohhhhhhhh. . . . yeah . . . yeah . . . fuck my brains out Russ . . . faster . . . Eeeeeaaaaaaaa . . . yes, Yes . . . YES . . . Ahhhhhhhh . . . "

Russ is unrelenting, perfectly happy and able to keep up with my demands. After twenty minutes of exhaustive stroking, Russ finally explodes into my depths, so powerfully that I gurgle, feeling as if his seed were gushing through me and out via my throat.

121

"No . . . no . . . no. . . . more . . . more . . . more . . . keep going. . . . please . . ."

Laughing, Russ explains, "All in good time, sweetie. Now we have to clean you out all over again."

Instead of refilling the douche bag, Russ reaches down to the base of the table next to where the retractable faucet is located. This time he brings up a retractable hose and nozzle, screwed directly into the plumbing. As he turns on the hot and cold water, a steady stream begins to flow from the nozzle. Once Russ is satisfied with the temperature and pressure, he inserts it and allows it to continuously clean and titillate me. I am in bliss as the gently pulsing waves repeatedly caress my ravaged interior.

"Okay, sweetie. I think we've outdone ourselves here. Let's move on. I'm getting antsy and those herbs have my cock twitching impatiently. I'm ready for the main event, now."

Oh God . . . main event? Russ removes the nozzle and turns off the water, slowly clicking the stirrups back to their original position. Then he releases the straps holding my feet and gets up to undo the handcuffs. Thankful for the momentary reprieve, I begin to move and stretch, getting the blood flowing back to all of my extremities. Russ helps me down from the table, and while doing so, playfully pinches my tightly clamped nipples. I gasp in surprise at their sensitivity, the ache rivaling a similar ache still building between my legs.

He leads me over to the table housing the stockade, but doesn't have me get up on it. Instead, he presses me up against it so that the edge creases my waist and then bends me over forward until my torso is lying flat on the table. My nipples are painfully pressed into the hard surface while the crystals dig themselves a cozy home in the underbelly of my soft breasts. Russ pulls my arms out well above my head and then flips up a set of wide, vinyl cuffs previously concealed beneath the table top. Once the cuffs are snapped into place, he opens them and locks my wrists inside, pinning me to the table. Another set of cuffs are flipped up and locked down, these to hold my biceps immobile. Lastly, my legs are pried apart and separated, the ankle of each strapped to a different leg of the table.

Russ begins to lovingly massage the cheeks of my ass, sighing as he grips and squeezes the fleshy mounds.

"Ah, at last. Do you remember the day of the poker game, Miranda . . . what I said to you when I first arrived at your house and saw you in that skimpy outfit? Do you remember what I said about your ass?"

"Mmmmhhhh, you said you were going to *have* it someday . . ."

"Someday is here, Miranda. This ass is now mine, and it will be mine for forty-eight more hours. I am going to use it over and over and over again."

"Oh, Russ . . . "

His erotic promise is too much . . . too much to handle in connection with the increasing inferno building in my pussy. My hips begin to gyrate and rub against the edge of the table, my frustration mounting when I realize that my clit will be left without stimulation. As hard as I try, I cannot get the edge of the table to rub anywhere near my throbbing button. Russ alternates between kissing and biting my ass, his lips and teeth touching every inch of my exposed bottom. Then he stands and moves away.

"I'll be right back."

Whimpering, I am abandoned, left to squirm helplessly on the cool, flat surface of the stark white table. I hear Russ moving about the sink area, much the same as before, the water running, rattling the bottles of herbs. Slowly but surely, my drug induced brain begins to figure out what's in store, as the sloshing sound from the douche bag once again reaches my ears.

"NO, Russ! Oh my God, NO! You can't do that, you just can't!"
   "Can't do what, darlin?"
   I begin to cry as I utter another feeble, "No . . . you just can't. . . ."
   "Poor, poor Miranda. You'll get used to it, I promise you. You may even grow . . . to like it."

Russ adjusts the stool height behind me so that his chest is level with my ass. Then he hangs the freshly mixed douche bag up on another pulley beside the table and sits down.
   Still unable to believe what he is about to do, I try to plead with him, but am unable to form a complete sentence.

"Russ . . . Russ . . . wait . . . you   can't. . . . why?. . . . how?. . . . Oh God, don't, please."

*   *   *

In response, I feel a slender nozzle begin to worm its way into my ass. NOOOOO!

It slips in smoothly and then widens, and then my ass closes tightly around it, securing it in place. Within seconds I feel the slow trickle of warm water begin to enter my bowels, terrifying me.

"What's the matter, Miranda? Hasn't Nick given you an enema before? No? I'm going to have to have a talk with that boy. He doesn't know what he's missing."

"Ruuuuuusssss . . . you're . . . sick."

"Thank you, but trying to sweet-talk me isn't going to get you out of this. I've been fantasizing about this moment for months, and I'm going to make it last. I've got the hose clamped down to the slowest trickle. It's probably going to take a good fifteen minutes to get this bag emptied into your gut. Hope you're comfortable. Now, what can I do to pass the time?"

Panicking, I hear Russ behind me, lowering his stool until I feel his tongue snake out and strike my clit, jolting me as if electrocuted.

"No reason why we can't make your first enema experience a pleasant one. Think I can get you off before the bag is empty?"

Racing to beat his own challenge, Russ begins to noisily slurp and lick at my pussy. His tongue is masterful, experienced, and despite the degradation being done to my ass, I begin to respond eagerly. My clit plumps up to the point of bursting, my hips bucking out and upward, inadvertently thrusting the enema nozzle slightly deeper. I begin to feel the familiar sensations creeping upward from my toes and the intense swirling in the pit of my stomach. Unable to hold back any longer, I cry out my release and attempt to quell the shudders rippling throughout my body, petrified that my convulsions will somehow expel the plug wedged tightly in my ass. Russ continues to lick and slurp up all the nectar my body has to offer, then stands to check on the progress of the bag.

"Almost done, sweetheart. Just a couple more minutes to go."

Panting in between breaths, I attempt to communicate with Russ.

"I. . . . feel. . . . full. . . . cramps . . . I   feel . . . cramping . . . "

Russ strokes my back while trying to reassure me.

"Shhhh, just relax. That's normal. It will pass more quickly if you relax. We're almost done now."

When Russ announces that the bag is finally empty, I feel about to explode. Mortified over how I'm going to be forced to eject the contents of my intestines, I begin to shake as Russ slowly removes the nozzle. Moving quickly to the side, he hollers, "Let it fly, baby!"

Fate is cruel and takes this moment to slow down the hands of time. Each second of this most degrading act. . . . the worst I've ever had to live through. . . . freezes, and then stretches into a minute, an hour . . . a day. The delay is interminable, my suffering, my humiliation extended so that I can remember and relive each and every moment with startling clarity. Thoughts of how I will ever survive this are interrupted by a warm spray of water coating my entire backside and legs. Realizing that my gut feels empty and the purge is over, I wait, trying to make myself as small as possible, wondering at Russ's reaction.

I have no reason to feel disgraced. Russ is jubilant. I couldn't have given him a better gift. Unable to conceive where this desire stems from, I just accept it as fact and pray to move on. Once Russ has everything cleaned back up again, he comes over to press a delighted kiss on the tip of my nose.

"Thank you for that indisputable display of surrender. Not like you had any choice. . . . but . . . "

Thinking the worst to be over, I ask Russ to unlatch me. Russ informs me, however, that I will be receiving two more enemas before I'll be released from the table, another cleansing enema, and then the final one containing milk and the ominous aphrodisiac herbs. Oh God . . . with the heat from those herbs still increasing in my pussy, how ever will I handle the same fire burning out of control in my ass?

I survive the second enema with a tad more dignity than the first, and am beginning to appreciate just how uplifting a cleaned out colon can feel. Not that I would like to repeat the procedure in such a humiliating way, but under the right circumstances, in the privacy of my own home, this treatment may prove to be quite beneficial. I wonder what Nick would think if I sprung that one on him? Jesus! Were Russ's perversions rubbing off onto me so quickly?

"Okay, honey. Your reward for being such a good girl. Here's the fun one. A nice, soothing milk enema laced with an itch. You're ass isn't going to know what hit it."

I am already envisioning myself fucking the wide end of a baseball bat just from the fury still unleashed in my pussy . . . what will happen once my ass has the same cravings? God help me. I begin to feel the warm milk flow into me, and with it an immediate heat. Soon the walls of my rear passage are twitching expectantly, waiting for a stimulation that will bring sweet relief. Russ plays with the nozzle a bit, pulling it completely out so that the milk and herb mixture will spill out, and therefore affect, my anus, then plunges it back to wreak havoc inside.

My hips thrust out as far as my bound body will allow, wanting to take on whatever is offered. Even the milk slowly filling my bottom becomes an object of relief, the sloshing providing tangible pleasure. Soon I am again begging Russ to ease the ache and take me, my wanton juices slowly dripping from my pussy to land in a puddle on the floor. Russ needs no further encouragement, the stimulation from the herbs still affecting his cock, as well as the display of my complete surrender. Russ moves in behind me and extra slowly begins to guide his cock into my searing pussy.

Knowing that he is far from having another orgasm, Russ develops a leisurely rhythm, with long, slow strokes. The effect is devastating, my entire body quivering in response. The milk, still slowly being pumped into my ass, caresses Russ's cock through the thin barrier separating my two passages. Russ is in heaven, holding my hips as he savors each stroke. I am in heaven, being used over and over and over again, as nothing other than a sex object.

When the enema bag is finally empty, Russ hesitates before removing the nozzle from my ass, contemplating his options.

"I think I'll stay just like this, slowly fucking you while I take out the nozzle. I know you're all cleaned out. There's nothing left in there but milk and herbs. Sounds like a perfect spa treatment."

"No, Russ, no. Haven't you humiliated me enough?"
    "Come on, don't fret. And once all the milk is out, as a reward, I'm going to shove my nice, thick cock into your delectable ass and fuck it for an hour. Won't that feel good, baby?"

Suddenly I am very impatient to expel the milk and herbs, the thought of Russ taking me as promised in his threats . . . disconcertingly appealing.
    "Yes . . . yes it will. Pull the plug, Russ. . . ."

Certain that there is no liquid left remaining in my gut, an elated Russ removes his prick from my pussy and begins to slowly work it into my ass. It slips in easily enough without additional lubrication, the interior walls of my bottom still coated with a light film of the mineral oil used in the previous two enemas. Russ and I moan simultaneously.

"Ooohhhhh God, Russ. . . . fuck it. . . . scratch that itch. . . . stretch me. . . . punish me . . ."

"Ooohhhhh God, Miranda. . . . finally, your ass is mine . . . sweeter than the sweetest of my dreams. . . . No, Miranda. . . . I'm taking my time . . . I'm going to enjoy your ass thoroughly . . . and slowly . . . "

"No . . . " I moan out softly, "It'll kill me . . . "

But it doesn't kill me. Russ enjoys my ass with long, slow strokes, and is true to his word. For over an hour, he determinedly sodomizes me with excruciatingly tantalizing plunges. Unable to do anything but receive, I quickly transform into a blubbering pile of Jell-o, one moment begging him to stop, the next begging him to go deeper, the next. . . . completely incoherent and unable to do anything but moan. Russ uses one hand to stimulate my clit during his relentless plundering of my bottom, bringing me to yet another orgasm. Through the haze, I try to recall how many times I've climaxed within the last twenty-four hours, but am unable to come up with a number. Just as Russ releases another surge of semen, this time into my rectum, I succumb to the darkness and mercifully pass out.

I awaken in a daze, staring up into an unfamiliar ceiling. What the . . . ? Where the hell am I? As I ask myself these questions, I attempt to roll over but find I am pinned down. Suddenly the events of last night come rushing back as I happen to focus on the giant wooden wheel. Russ.

---

*   *   *

"Morning buttercup. I trust you slept well."

Oh God. I turn my head in his direction. He is smiling cheerfully, carrying a plate of delicious smelling breakfast.

"Hungry? Wouldn't want my beautiful captive to starve. You're going to need all of your energy and then some."

"What happened?"

"Last night?" Russ begins, as he takes a seat beside me. "Well. . . ." he goes on to explain through large bites of eggs and hash browns, "You passed out. Just as I blew my wad into your tight little ass. Out like a light. Kind of rude, if you ask me. Now, if I were a mean person, I would have revived you just so you could suffer through a sleepless night. . . . those herbs still going strong. I would have tied you down to this bondage bed wide awake, and then left you to moan and squirm and want. But, I decided that I'd rather have you fully rested so that you could keep up with me today. There'll be plenty of time to let you suffer later."

"Oh how chivalrous."

"Yeah, you'll be on your hands and knees later . . . kissing my feet . . . and eating those words, baby. Go ahead. Be a smart ass while you can."

I watch in amazement as Russ woofs down the last of his food.

"Hey! I thought you were going to feed me some. You just ate it all!"

"Yours is upstairs, honey, keeping warm. You've got

a few things to do first before you can eat."

Oh, no . . . here we go again. "Like what?" I ask, somewhat resigned.

"Hmmm. . . . just some general hygiene."

The pure glee in his eyes contradicts the matter-of-fact manner in which he utters the innocent sounding statement.

"I just bet you need to use the restroom again, don't you?"

"Nnnnnnooooo, Russ, don't make me do that again, please. Isn't once enough?"

"Miranda, by the time you leave here Monday morning, it'll be second nature to you. Do you understand?"

"Why?! What is it that gets you so off about that? It's gross. It's disgusting."

"*That* is what gets me *so off*, Miranda. The fact that you find it so horrifying. I get a charge out of making you do things that appall you. It's a power trip, really. Revenge for what you put me through the last nine months."

"That was the last book."

"What?"

"Never mind. So . . . what you're telling me . . . is that . . . if I enjoyed urinating in front of you, you wouldn't feel the desire to make me do it?"

"No, what I'm telling you is . . . once you become comfortable with it, I'll change it in some way so that you find it distressing again."

"God damn it, Russ, you're an asshole."

"Yesterday, I was Mr. Nice Guy. . . . today. . . ."

* * *

Russ never finishes his sentence, preferring to allow me to come up with my own conclusions. Instead, he leans down and begins to release me from the bondage bed.

"First, I need you to call Nick and make up some excuse as to why you need to be away for the weekend. Then . . . we're going to go play on the seesaw ladder."

Nick accepts my lame excuse of a needy friend without too much difficulty, his immediate problem of having to deal with his hangover outweighing any suspicions he may have had about my whereabouts. Satisfied, Russ leads me over to the ladder and fastens me face down, probably three feet above the floor. My arms are bound to the sides of the padded ladder running above my shoulders and upward, the tips of my fingers almost reaching the mirrored wall. One of the horizontal rungs hits me at about my collar bone, the second at my rib cage, and the third, right at my hips. There are no more horizontal rungs below my hips. My legs are pulled outward and around, draping the exterior of the ladder as much as my flexibility will allow, and then fastened there securely with straps. Then Russ begins to raise the ladder up, until I can see the top of his head. The sensation is frightening, almost as if I could fall, even though I know that to be quite impossible.

"I . . . I . . . thought you were going to let me go to the bathroom first, Russ."

"And you thought correctly, sweetums. Hang on a second. I'll be right back."

* * *

Oh God . . . oh God . . . oh God. . . . What's he going to do? I begin to panic. Russ comes back with the nipple clamps I had been wearing the night before and two matching devices that remind me of spatulas. Russ walks under my levitated body with ease, and begins to fasten the nipple clamps. This time there are no soft kisses, no foreplay, no preparation . . . just a cruel, heartless pinch and then Zzziiiinnnggggggggggg.

"Aaaahhhhhhhhhhhhh . . . " I groan out in discomfort.

Russ attaches the other clamp, watching as my nipples get pulled downward from the weight of the crystals. The pain is bearable but not quite as pleasurable as the previous night. Then, in surprise, I watch as Russ attaches *another* crystal to the bottom of each one, yanking my nipples even further down.

"Owwwwwwww, Owwwwwwwww, Russ, Russ, that really hurts. Please, take them off."

Laughing, Russ replies, "Miranda, Miranda, Miranda. Your naivete is so sweet and appealing, that I'll tell you what. I won't remove them, but I'll do something that will help you find them more. . . . titillating."

Russ again walks away, this time in the direction of his sink and cabinet. He returns holding a tube of cream. Standing under me while looking up into my face, he explains, "This cream is made from those same herbs you found so stimulating last night."

Russ squeezes some onto his fingers and then begins to apply it to my nipples. Once both nipples are covered, he continues to rub the cream into the entire breast, leaving no patch of the delicate skin untouched. My breasts immediately begin to tingle and throb, the weight of the crystals no longer painful. As a matter of fact, I resist the urge to beg Russ to add a third . . .

"Is that better, baby?"

"Oooohhhh yes, yes . . . much better."

Chuckling evilly, Russ replies, "For now."

Russ wanders back over to the sink area, and I listen with dread as he prepares the horrid pink bag. Thinking that I will receive the douche first, I cry out in surprise when I feel the small nozzle enter my ass instead. Then directly following it, I feel a larger nozzle coaxing my sleepy nether lips apart and slowly penetrate until it is well encased within the satiny walls of my pussy. Why does it come as such a surprise that Russ has two bags?

I feel the warm liquids begin to flow into their respective channels and swirl around, bringing with them the potent effects of the diabolical herbs. Whimpering, I can only let it happen, unable to stop the vindictive turn Russ's game has taken.

Russ moves aside and begins to remove his sweat pants. When he is completely nude, he grabs the two white spatulas and lies down on the floor beneath me, facing upward, only I am looking at his knees while his head is positioned between my widespread legs at the other end. Russ flips a switch on the floor, and the ladder begins to lower, stopping when I am only six inches away from his threatening body.

Russ has both bags clamped on the lowest trickle, but I am already beginning to feel water spurt out from my

135

pussy, dribbling down to land on Russ's chest. I begin to panic anew as my filling cavities begin to put pressure on my painfully full bladder. Whack!

"Ow! What was that for?"

"Let's see how long you can hold out. I'm going to smack both of your ass cheeks with these paddles until you piss on me."

"Oh God . . . you want me to piss *on* you now? Oh God . . ."

Even though Russ's position doesn't allow him to get any strength behind the swats landing on my bottom, he is quick and repetitive, all the stinging smacks falling exactly in the same location. Within five minutes, the cheeks of my ass are smarting, my gut is full, my rectum's on fire, my pussy's on fire, my tits are on fire, and I've relieved myself all over Russ's chest. All I can think about is how I'm going to kill him when I'm finally let free. The ladder begins to raise as Russ scoots out from under it, stopping it at waist high. Then he removes both nozzles and stands back to view the rest my demeaning expulsion. Again, the hose is turned on and the floor and my backside are rinsed clean of any evidence of foul play. Finally, I am released from the ladder and carried over to the tub.

Russ accompanies me into the tub, turning on the shower and giving me a good scrub down. Reluctantly, he removes the nipple clamps and washes away most of the cream from my breasts. No area of my body is left untouched, even the washing of my hair. When I am completely clean, he takes care of his own needs, seeing to every crack and crevice. Finally, I am towel dried and guided over to the large, wooden wheel.

It is hard to concentrate as Russ gives me instructions, my need to hump something growing stronger and more persistent. My whole body is alive and waiting . . . for something . . . for anything. I am a huge mass of desire, craving any kind of attention. Russ smiles in satisfaction at my discomfort, somehow knowing the tortures I feel.

Again I find myself inside the huge wooden wheel. Russ asks me to spread my legs as far apart as possible, and then begins to fasten soft leather cuffs to my ankles and wrists. Once the cuffs are in place, rope is threaded through an eyelet on each one and then out through the wooden slats, knotted together on the outer side of the wheel. Russ has to use a ladder to fasten my arms to the top of the wheel, a small price to pay for the end result. When he is done, I am tethered to the wheel, spread-eagled, as wide as my arms and legs can possibly be forced apart.

The intense burning in my two most private orifices is not enough to console a bitter Russ, and he leaves to retrieve the tube of magic cream that he had used on my nipples and breasts earlier. He also has with him the frightening nipple clamps. He sets to work massaging the cream into my breasts once again, but doesn't stop there. He goes lower, coating my ribcage, belly and thighs, then to the rear, attacking my buttocks and back with the doctored balm. He makes sure that my anus and pussy are generously attended to, then stands to rub the remaining cream on the lips of my mouth. I howl in pure sufferance, my body begging for appeasement.

"Time for your breakfast, toots. I'll be right back."

"Russ . . . please, do something. I need to be touched. Don't just leave me here to suffer."

Russ only smiles, returning with another plate of piping hot food and begins to hand feed me.

"Eat slowly . . . wouldn't want you getting a tummy ache."

I find that I am ravenous and soon have all the yummy eggs and shredded potatoes devoured. I continue to lick my mouth far after all tidbits of food are gone, the pressure against my drugged lips too sensual to resist. After the distraction of breakfast has passed, my neglected body again begins to demand attention.

"Russ. . . . please . . . now. . . . touch me. My body is aching . . . on fire . . ."

"As you wish."

Russ walks on over to the cabinet housing the whips and paddles. I begin to tremble with anticipation, thankful for any type of reprieve, even a painful one. Russ brings back a cat-o-nine tails and a riding crop and then asks me where I'd like to feel it first.

"Oh God . . . my breasts."

The cat is whisked briskly across my breasts, tearing from me a scream of ecstatic agony.

"Yyyyyyyeeessss . . . Again . . . !"

Not one to deny his lady captives, Russ keeps the whip moving in time with my demands.

"Ahhhhhh. . . . more. . . . my stomach. . . . YES! . . . my thighs . . . my thighs next. . . . Oooooh God . . . again . . . harder . . . Yes . . . Again . . . Again . . . faster Russ . . . whip me . . . everywhere . . . Oh MY GOD . . . "

The whip keeps flying, although Russ remains very much in control and does not allow any one spot to be abused. The biting strands of the whip feel heavenly against my excited body, soothing and tormenting all at once. My arousal intensifies with each lash, and I cloudily wonder if I'll somehow be brought to the point of a masochistic orgasm.

"My back now, Russ. . . . my ass. . . . whip my ass. . . . yes, oh yes . . . Mmmmmm. . . . Eeeeeowwww. . . . Ooooooo . . . more . . . the back of my thighs . . . God damn you, Russ, for doing this to me . . . Ahhhhhhhhhh. . . . keep going . . . again . . . "

When my body has a nice rosy glow from shoulders to knees, Russ stops the whipping, only to have me squirming and mewling for more.

"Sorry, Miranda . . . I want you tenderized, not filleted. This is all for now. I've got more treats in store for you. You won't go without. . . . for a while, that is."

* * *

My moans are pathetic, pleading . . . but Russ appears immune.

"Time to cool you off a bit. How about some ice for those sore, hot nipples?"

Out of nowhere, Russ's hand appears with a cube of ice. He slowly places it on the tip of my left nipple and begins to rub it around, watching my nipple bloom around the meltdown. When my nipple seems to raise up as taut as possible, on goes the nipple clamp, complete with two dangling crystals. I suck in my breath and grit my teeth, as I become accustomed to the severe sensations ripping through my torso. Ice and the adjoining clamp are applied to my other nipple, and soon I am gasping in painful delight as I pull and struggle against my unyielding restraints.

Russ steps back to admire his handiwork, and then starts to singsong:

> "Miranda loves to tease . . .
> Now I'll use her as I please. . . .
> Her fate rests in my hands . . .
> Miranda loves to flirt . . .
> I so crave to watch her hurt . . .
> She'll fulfill all my demands . . ."

"Ohhhhhhhh . . . Russ . . ."
"Hot . . . cold . . . hot. . . . cold. . . . guess it's time for hot again, sweetie."

Russ goes over to his whip and paddle case and opens a drawer. He pulls out two strange looking candles and a book of matches. I watch apprehensively as he walks back toward me and sets one of them down. Each candle looks like two candles fused together in the center by a flat, oval base. One end of the candle is black and quite phallic looking, while the other half is cherry red and in the shape of your typical candle. One candle is also slightly thinner than the other. I shudder, already aware of where the candles are going to end up.

Russ lights the red end of one of the candles and steps up next to me in the wheel. He grasps my hair with one hand and pulls my head back to keep my face from being scorched as he places the candle a few inches above one breast and then angles it to drip directly onto my already tortured nipple. I screech as the first drop of wax lands to encase my nipple, several more soon to follow. Russ doesn't stop until the top and sides are completely entombed in several layers of wax. He moves to the other side and covers that nipple as well, sheathing it in a casket of red.

When he is content with his artwork, he blows out the candle, lets go of my hair and steps from the wheel. Then, he releases a lever and the wheel slowly begins to rotate. I panic as I am thrown off balance, but my cuffs are held secure and I stay in place, even though the weight of my body begins to shift. Soon I am completely upside down, crying out once again as the crystals from the clamps topple over, wrenching my nipples from a new angle. Some of the wax begins to crack, but miraculously stays put. Russ once again lights the red end of the candle and bends down to finish covering the under side of each nipple. When he is done, he takes the still lit candle and moves it between my wide open legs.

Without so much as a warning, I feel the penis-shaped bottom half of the candle being inserted into my honey-drenched cavern, helping to ease the fires raging within. I can feel the heat from the flame as it spreads outward, warming the insides of my thighs. Afraid to even breathe, I watch in horror as Russ picks up the second candle and walks around to the back of the wheel. Before long, I feel the shapely head of that candle commence to worm its way deep into the warm sleeve of my ass, and then the heat to emanate as Russ maliciously lights the accompanying wick.

"My . . . God. . . . Russ. . . . what are you doing?" I whisper, afraid to even raise my voice.

"Just a little mind fuck, Miranda. Are you scared that I'm going to let you burn?"

"Yeeeeesssss. . . . Oh please, Russ . . . this is dangerous. Blow them out . . . please!"

"Not quite yet. I've got a few things I want you to do for me before I do. Just don't move too much, and you shouldn't have any problems."

Russ begins to laugh out loud at that suggestion and wanders away. I, on the other hand, am immersed in sensory overload. The blood has begun rushing to my head, making me quite woozy. My body is still craving stimulation . . . of any kind, itching to be touched, prodded, poked . . . anything. The flames burning treacherously close to my thighs and my most intimate areas are petrifying me, yet I cannot help but to squeeze wantonly at the devices responsible for holding them in place. Please . . . if I can just keep myself from moving.

Any hope of remaining still is immediately dashed as Russ returns carrying with him a bag of clothespins and a heavy duty vibrator.

"Now, sweetness. I want you to shower me with praise, and I want you to make it believable. I'm going to put clothespins all over your body, and after each one, say something nice about me. If. . . . you do a good job, I'll let you cum and then blow out the candles. If. . . . you don't. . . . your cunt, ass and thighs will suffer. Ready?"

Russ begins clamping the pins to my already inflamed skin, his first area of concentration being my quivering belly. Desperate for the attack to end, I shout out anything and everything that comes to mind.

"Oh God Russ . . . you know how to please a woman . . . what turns her on. You have the best cock . . . the best fuck around. Sssssssssssssssss. . . ."

I try to keep up with Russ's momentum, but he is applying the clothespins much too quickly. Soon my belly and thighs have wooden legs sticking out from all angles, and he moves around back to repeat the damage. Unable to keep my body from jerking as Russ attaches the pins, I soon have hot wax splattering against the tender skin of my inner thighs. I begin to screech as each little fireball lands, some now dripping onto the lips of my pussy and all over my crotch area. Even my clit is not to be spared, wrenching from me another scream of anguish.

"Miranda . . . you've stopped talking. Keep talking or you're going to lose."

"Ruuuuusssss . . . you are masterful . . . and so. . . . hand . . . some . . . Eeeeeeeee . . . those blue . . . eyes . . . can melt a glacier . . . and your kisses . . . are hypnotic . . . I crave them . . . I want to be kissed . . . Ooouuuch . . . by you . . . Ohhhhhh . . . over . . . and over again. Your body is beautiful . . . muscular and sooooooooo owwwww . . . strong. . . . please Russ. . . . stop now . . . "

"More."

"You are so sssssmmmmmart. . . . eeeeechhhh . . . and patient . . . and . . . "

Russ stops with the clothespins and picks up the vibrator, coming back to the front to place it directly on my swollen clit. He turns it up full blast sending several jolts through my body, my muscles now in constant spasm. Russ blows out the candles for the remainder of this torture, the hot wax still being thrown in all directions as my shuddering body reacts to this new stimuli.

"Ok . . . you cock-teasing bitch . . . now, when you start to cum, I want you to say. . . . *Master Russ, I adore you. You rule my sex.*"

Already feeling the beginning pulses of my approaching orgasm, I scream out . . . "Mmmmaster Ruuusss. . . . I yeyeyeyeee . . . a . . . a . . . adddd . . . adddore . . . you. . . . Yyyyou . . . rrrruuule. . . . mmmy. . . . ssssSEXXXX!"

My body collapses in a fit of convulsions while Russ turns off the vibrator and slowly begins to rotate the wheel so that I am positioned upright. In danger of losing consciousness, I struggle to keep aware, concentrating on my breathing as the blood quickly drains from my face. I don't even notice the pain in my nipples as the crystals are flipped around, and then released, as Russ removes the clamps entirely. The clothespins quickly follow suit, as well as the candles, until I am left void of stimulation, only the patches of caked-on wax remaining to remind me of my ordeal.

"Was it like I promised, Miranda? Did heaven and hell collide? Are you able to tell the difference, baby . . . or *is* hell. . . . heaven?"

Russ exits the room entirely, leaving me alone to contemplate my predicament. My body is still too exhausted to react to the effect of the herbs, a tiny blessing, but my brain and my thoughts are still quite active. Russ is definitely agitated today, a big change in his demeanor from yesterday. Yesterday, he seduced me. Today he's terrorizing me. The end results, however, are both the same. . . . mind-altering exhilaration. I can't remember my body feeling this alive, thriving on the endless stimulation, pulsing with anticipation. Is this going to be Russ's true revenge . . . exposing and igniting these masochistic cravings, only to release me knowing my need to return will soon fester into an undeniable obsession?

Hours must have passed before a stark naked Russ saunters back into the room, sporting a fierce erection and a wild gleam in his eyes. My arms and legs are dreadfully sore, and I silently plea that Russ's first order of business will be to release me. Unfortunately, Russ has his own ideas. Russ takes his right hand and wraps it around his erection as he walks closer, masturbating to the sight of my spread-out body.

"How are you feeling, baby?" Russ asks, with exaggerated sweetness. "Getting a little bit tired of holding that pose? Somebody has been thinking about you for a while and would like to show you how much."

Referring to his penis, he looks down as he continues to casually stroke himself. Then he steps up into the wheel to stand directly in front of me and begins to pick up the pace, increasing the friction on his rigid prick.

"Oooooo, baba. . . . he likes what he sees. Oh yes . . . oh yes. . . . his horny slut, spread out and waiting for him. He finds that so exciting. Look . . . he's starting to cry, he's so happy . . ."

Now Russ starts to gently slap his cock up against my belly . . . Ooooing and Ahhhhhing the whole time while sucking air between his clenched teeth.

"Oh yes. . . . he's going to kiss you here in a minute . . . "

Russ stops the cock spanking and resumes stroking, pumping his hand up and down much faster while his other hand cradles his balls.

"Oooooo . . . Mirandaaaaa . . .
AAAAAAARRRRRRGGGGGGHHHHH!"

Russ aims the powerful spurts of his hot, creamy cum directly at my slit, bestowing me with that kiss that he

---

had promised just moments ago. When the last of his load is deposited between my pouting lips, he takes the head of his still erect cock and begins to rub it around the folds of my pussy. My body reacts automatically, instinctively, and my hips begin to thrust outward, inviting the object of my lust to enter. Enter it does . . . swiftly, fluidly, sensually . . . taking on its own identity as it begins it's sumptuous rhythm.

I begin to coo. . . . purr . . . at the delightful impalement, feeling every pulsing throb beating in his masculine shaft. He reaches around to hold me tightly, then descends those luscious lips to meld with mine. I sigh in heavenly bliss at the return of the erotic, gentle master, wooing his captive into submissiveness rather than resorting to coercion. Lost in his kiss, I could promise him anything.

Russ leisurely fucks me while his lips remain locked with my own. His arms and hands are constantly roving, alternating between gripping my ass and caressing my breasts, coaxing contented sighs from my gurgling throat. After several minutes, he withdraws and picks up the tube of herbal cream still left lying nearby. He moves behind me and coats my anus with the powerful aphrodisiac, then slips his finger inside to lubricate the interior as well. When his finger is removed, it is replaced by the wide berth of his cock head pressing anxiously against my rear opening. His arms wrap around to hug me, his fingers settling into the folds of my pussy. Pushing past my tight barrier, he gasps out in pleasure, methodically enjoying all the taboo delights my ass has to offer. I sway in my bondage against him, two of his fingers rhythmically penetrating my pussy in sync with his precise thrusting into my bottom. His other hand rubs and massages my clit, until my toes are curling and I'm caught in the throes of another passionate orgasm. Russ is only moments behind me, releasing a flood of his seed deep into my irresistible ass.

"Would you find it exciting to exist as you are now, on a day to day basis, as nothing more than a sexy receptacle. . . . no worries, no cares, no responsibilities . . . your sole purpose being to bring me pleasure?"

Thank goodness he didn't ask me that question while wrapped in his embrace and smothered by his kisses.

"No, Russ . . . I wouldn't. I find it . . . exciting, to say the least . . . for the weekend. But as a way of life. . . . I would hate it."

Smiling good-naturedly, Russ responds with, "Hmmm . . . I'm not so sure. Weekends quickly blend into weeks . . . weeks into months . . . months into years . . . years into lifetimes. You'd be so engrossed that time would have no meaning for you. You'd be too busy *feeling* to bother with the passage of time."

"Russ . . ." I question, warily, "You're not thinking about reneging on your promise to return me home Monday morning, are you? Nick isn't stupid. He'll figure out where I am and come after you."

"No, no, no . . . just giving you food for thought."

"Thanks, but no thanks . . . I'm on a very strict diet."

Grinning, Russ shoots me a look that says, "Can't blame a guy for trying."

* * *

By nightfall, I am completely worn out. Russ has to physically drag me over to my bed, my limbs no longer able to hold my weight. He only attaches one ankle to the bottom of the bed, deciding that anything further won't be necessary, since he will be sleeping right beside me.

"Is it customary for kidnappers to sleep with their captives?" I ask him, with sarcastic innocence.

"Baby . . . I just do what feels good at the time. Right now I want nothing more than to snuggle up to your hot and inviting body and hold it against me all night long."

"Geesh. This is beginning to feel like a relationship . . ." I mutter, under my breath.

Morning arrives, and with it a rejuvenated Russ, eager to spring more of his surprises on me. I sit up on the bed and watch him as he prepares for my morning ritual, keeping a special eye out for the bottle containing the aphrodisiac herbs. I watch as he uses it, carefully measuring the powdered herbs before shaking them into the pink bags, relieved that I can now distinguish that bottle from the others. Russ wanders over to the seesaw ladder and hooks both bags up to pulleys, then hoists them way up near the ceiling. I look on with interest as my curiosity increases, never before being allowed to witness the time-consuming routine. Once everything is in place, Russ releases my ankle from the bondage bed and steers me over to the ladder.

I am placed lying face down again, only this time, Russ angles the ladder so that I am perpendicular to the floor, the top of my head aimed at the floor and my feet toward the ceiling.

"What are you doing? Why do you want me upside down?"

"I have something extra special in mind for you today. I want those herbs to stay put in that luscious pussy of yours for a while and not seep out. That cunt is going to need to be hungry and juicy."

"Jesus, Russ . . . what are you going to do to me?"

"Only time will tell, precious, now relax."

We complete the entire regime . . . the douche, the enema, the shower, and then Russ grabs the herb cream and walks back over to the bondage bed. With a sleepy, inviting smile, he pats the bed, indicating for me to join him.

"I thought you had something special in mind. What are we going to do, make out on the bed?"

"Have I lied to you yet? Come lay beside me."

Confused, I do as requested, lying flat on my back and looking up at him with suspicion. He simply grins as he undoes the cap to the tube and begins to massage the vilely wonderful cream onto my breasts and down into that sacred area between my legs. I shudder, knowing how the cream will affect me, combined with the added potency of my special douche. Russ tosses the tube aside and then leans down, pressing his body, off centered, to cover only the right half of mine.

He kisses me and tenderly strokes my body for almost a half an hour, never once touching my pussy in the process. My hips are bucking upward, my opening frothing with unquenched desire.

"My God, Russ . . . if you don't do something soon, I'm going to die! You're driving me crazy!"

As if on cue, Russ's hand slides down to nestle between my legs.

"Oh, baby . . . you're so wet, but I don't know if you're wet enough. I'll be right back."

The howl that follows him is pathetic as my own hands dive downward to help ease some of the torment. My fingers provide some relief, however temporary, until Russ returns, carrying with him a large container of petroleum jelly. His gaze is intense, and his eyes never waver from mine as he dips into the jar and begins to grease up his entire right hand. His look dares me to protest as he continues spreading the slippery substance up his forearm, stopping at his elbow. Certain that he is adequately covered, he lays back down and begins to taunt me.

"Ever been fisted, baby? Do you know what it feels like to have someone's entire hand and wrist buried to the hilt in your most intimate passages?"

I shake my head no, never breaking eye contact, frozen in awe at his suggestion. The thought all at once petrifies me, yet is responsible for another surge of moisture sent to saturate my already flooded sex. I groan with expectancy as Russ's fingers resume their position between my legs and attempt the improbable.

Russ easily slips three fingers inside and begins an in and out thrusting motion. I exhale slowly, drowning in the exquisite sensations, my feminine juices overflowing and mixing with the Vaseline. Encouraged by the ease in which the three fingers entered, Russ slyly slips in his pinky, making it four. Then tucking his thumb under, be begins to slowly gain entry using all five fingers. The process is painstakingly slow, the most difficult part of it being to get past the last knuckle on his thumb. Finally, after much kissing and coaxing on his part for me to relax, that obstacle is overcome and his hand begins to slowly disappear inside. Amazed, Russ sits up, needing to verify his success with his own two eyes.

I feel Russ's fingers curl as they make a fist inside, creating additional room for more of his arm to enter. I am thunderstruck, unable to speak, never undergoing such an intimidating and breathtaking experience. This feeling of total consummation and ultimate vulnerability exceed anything I have ever imagined. It is almost too personal, too giving of an emotion to happen with someone like Russ. This should be Nick's fist inside me. Too late to turn back, I give in, gasping as Russ slowly begins to plunge the entire first third of his arm in and out of me. I try to crawl out of my skin, arching backwards, the overwhelming sensations too much for my battered mind and body to handle. Russ holds fast, wriggling his fingers in an attempt to bring me more pleasure. I scream out in ecstasy as a catastrophic orgasm cruelly rips through me, the walls of my pussy clenching and suffocating Russ's invading fist.

*   *   *

When the spasms subside, I begin to worry irrationally
. . . how in the world is he going to be able to remove
his fist? He's going to rip me to shreds in the process. I
begin to hyperventilate as this new fear nags at my consciousness.

"Baby . . . baby . . . it's okay . . . relax. You're okay.
Take a deep breath and hold it. Shhhhhhhhhhh."
"Russ . . . I'm scared. . . . it's never going to come out.
Your fist is going to be trapped inside. Oh my God . . . "
"Miranda, Miranda, Miranda. . . . calm down, baby.
It'll come out, no problem, but you can't overreact and
tense up on me like this. You have to relax, get all warm
and gushy . . . like butta baby. . . . like butta."

His voice is like "butta," immediately lulling me back
into a state of tranquil arousal, hypnotic, drugged. Something about being around Russ always makes me feel
woozy, like I'm not in my right mind, under the influ-
ence of a powerful narcotic or something.
Before I am even aware that it has happened, he holds
his wet and sloppy hand up for my inspection.
"See, I told you . . . nothing to worry about, darling."

"Hungry?"
"Famished. Finally going to feed me?"
Russ has the decency to blush. "Well, I kind of got
sidetracked this morning. I'll be right back with some
fruit. Don't you go anywhere, kitten."

Russ returns with a couple of bananas and a bowl of cut
up melon. We devour the succulent slices of cantaloupe

and honeydew first, and then Russ peels a banana and holds it up to my lips. I open my mouth to take a bite, but Russ pulls it away, content to lightly brush the tip of the banana across my bottom lip. Leaving my mouth partially held open, I hold still while he finishes playing out his current fantasy.

"Lick your lips and open them a little wider."

I do as he asks, and he immediately begins to penetrate my mouth with the top inch of the banana, slowly guiding it in and out. The simple act seems to fascinate him as he thrusts it in a little deeper.

"Fuck it. Fuck it with your mouth. Use your tongue. Get it squishy."

Russ is enthralled as he watches me take the banana as I would a penis. Soon the banana begins to soften and Russ's anxiety increases.

"Deep throat it. Keep your hands behind your back. Just take it as I give it to you."

Keeping my fingers tightly laced behind my back, I open up a little wider, expanding my throat and mentally psyching myself up to not gag. Soon I feel the persistent pressure, beyond my vocal cords, pressing further back and down. I begin to bite off mushy pieces of banana, not with my teeth, but with the contractions in my throat, quickly swallowing the tiny globs before I choke on them. Russ force feeds me most of the banana in this fashion, remaining very thoughtful throughout the whole process. He saves the last two inches of the banana for himself, chewing it down properly. Then Russ offers me a drink of orange juice, and I gulp it down gratefully.

"This just gave me an idea. Follow me."

Russ takes my hand and all but drags me back over into the white section of the room. He orders me up onto the white table on my hands and knees and then encases my head and arms in the white stockade. Then he flips up the side shackles and pins my legs to the table just below my knees, spreading my legs obscenely wide. I feel very defenseless in this doggy-style position, the stockade and shackles making it even more pronounced. But the herbs are still working, my body continuously craving attention, and my ass wiggles back at Russ in anticipation.

"That's my girl," he laughs, as he wanders back over to the bondage bed to retrieve the remaining banana.

My body immediately begins to tingle and my pussy clenches invitingly, certain that the banana will soon be finding its way inside. What is Russ going to do, insert it and then eat it out of me? The thought is definitely appealing, but my thoughts change instantly when Russ shows me the altered banana. Russ uses a knife to saw off the very top, leaving about a quarter-size opening. The rest of the banana remains securely in its peel, and then Russ makes a show out of coating it entirely with Vaseline. Next, Russ moves behind me, and I am held fast by the stockade, forced to look straight ahead into the wooden room.

I begin to struggle profusely as I feel the newly altered banana top pressing against my anal opening, but my efforts only succeed in amusing Russ.

* * *

"Baby, you can't go anywhere. You just have to kneel there and take it. Take whatever it is I want you to. And right now.... I want it to be this banana."

Gradually, Russ works the head of the banana past my tight barrier and slides it in deep, coating the walls of my rectum with the petroleum jelly. With exaggerated slowness he penetrates and then pulls it all the way back out, and then starts all over again, cruelly toying with my rear opening. The banana is fairly large, and I gasp as I try to relax enough to accommodate it comfortably. Russ picks up the tempo now, no longer removing it completely, thrusting into me deeply and quickly. My moans increase with intensity and are soon filling the room. Not quite ready to allow me another orgasm, Russ backs off, leaving only the first inch of the banana imbedded.

"Let me know when you feel something, baby."

Confused, I try to decipher his meaning, when all of a sudden I feel the walls of my ass expanding.

"Oh my God, Russ, what are you doing?"
"Just inserting a little lubricant, darling."

Mortified, I can do nothing but accept the fact that little by little, Russ is squeezing the entire banana out of its peel and into my ass. I cringe as I feel it filling my bottom, certain the end result will be nothing less than another unbearable humiliation. Russ leaves the peel hanging limply from my ass as he crawls up onto the table and situates himself on his knees between my out-stretched thighs. He then simultaneously slips the peel out while pressing the head of his cock inside. I feel as if I'm going to burst as Russ penetrates my bottom and begins to slice through my banana coated interior. The moans coming from him tell me that the sensations for him are incredible, yet I continue to struggle with my own discomfort. Russ takes care of that immediately, reaching a hand around to manipulate my clit while he continues to fuck me from behind. The magic of his fingers quickly transforms me from passive victim to eager participant, and I begin to involuntarily thrust back.

"Oh yes, baby. Fuck me back. Take it all. You are such a sweet fuck . . . a sweet, receptive fuck. Come on . . . do me. . . . let's make some banana cream . . . fuck it."

Russ smacks my ass while urging me on via his erotic ranting, sending sizzling shivers throughout my body. The harder and longer Russ continues to plunge into me, the more liquefied the banana becomes, easing the bloated feeling I had initially. The rutting intensifies, our groans co-mingling, as the room begins to swirl and then constrict into a tiny dot of light. I feel my ears start to tingle and then go deaf, my nipples harden, and then suddenly I am there, immersed in feeling, every nerve the recipient of unparalleled ecstasy, as I miraculously climax at unimaginable heights, convulsing and shuddering into a pool of elated bliss. Two strokes later, Russ becomes lost in his own climactic spasms, collapsing in a heap across my back. It is sprawled out in this position that my husband walks in to find us.

CHAPTER 7

∎

COMPLICATIONS

My eyes widen in shock, then horror as Nick steps out from behind a concealed door built into one of the mirrored walls.

"Ok . . . the party's over. Time for me to take her home."

"Hey, man. You said I could have her till Monday morning."

"I know what I said, but I've changed my mind. You've had plenty of time and enjoyed plenty of kink with my wife. No need to feel shortchanged."

I watch in bewilderment as Russ jumps down from the table and joins Nick on the other side of the room. My fury mounts as they begin to whisper.

"Will somebody get me down from this table and tell me what the FUCK is going on here?!!!!" I bellow, quickly gaining the attention of both men.

*   *   *

Russ guiltily races back to release me, while Nick stares me down, not at all daunted by the fact that I'm quite pissed off. I jump down off of the table, ready to do battle, when I am reminded that I still have banana oozing from my bottom and am in no condition to demand an explanation.

"I need to shower before I go anywhere. Are those clothes for me?"

Nick has a pair of sweats draped over his arm and tosses them in my direction. Then he and Russ leave the dungeon and head up the stairs to do some talking, leaving me with my privacy. Livid, I step into the shower and scrub myself clean, certain that my husband is the mastermind behind my abduction. How could he have done this to me? As I am getting dressed, I happen to spy the brown jar containing the special herbs sitting on Russ's counter. I quickly scan the room to make sure no one is around, then impulsively stuff the jar into the pocket of my hooded sweatshirt, not knowing what I intend to use them for, but confident they will come in handy someday. Then, taking the stairs two at a time, I enter Russ's kitchen ready for a confrontation.

Russ had the decency to at least get into a pair of sweatpants before I had to make eye contact with him again. I walk in to find he and Nick sitting, chatting amiably and drinking coffee at his kitchen table. Flabbergasted, I reiterate, "Does somebody want to tell me what's going on?"

*　　*　　*

"Sure," Russ offers, "Nick gave you to me for the week-end."

"You're not helping, buddy," Nick counters. "It's not quite that simple, Miranda. Have a seat and I'll fill you in."

Feeling unforgivably betrayed, I sit down with my arms crossed and wait for an explanation.

"As you know," Nick begins, "Russ has felt slighted ever since the poker game. It was beginning to affect our friendship, which wasn't something I had expected. In an effort to appease him, I suggested that he send you e-mails in an attempt to try and seduce you."

"You told him to write those creepy poems?" I ask, accusingly.

"No. I didn't tell him what to say. I just gave him your e-mail address. He came up with that tactic all on his own. Regardless, his initial poems didn't work, so he decided to mess with your head by using the *expect it when you least expect it* method. All that did was freak you out, but when you admitted to me that it turned you on, Russ and I got together and arranged the *rape*, so to speak."

"Nick! How could you? I'm your wife, for crying out loud. How could you do such a thing?"

"You're not letting me finish. I told Russ that I'd help to get you out to the baseball field, but that before he could take you by force, he had to get your permission. I never expected you to say, 'yes,' but I had no idea how cleverly Russ was going to manipulate the situation. Plain and simply, I underestimated him, and he out-smarted me. Once he had your 'ok,' all I could do was sit back and watch to make sure that he didn't get carried away."

"You watched us? The whole time? How?"

"Well, it was easy to watch while you were blindfolded, and then I just stood behind you after the blindfold was removed. When Russ decided to leave, I ran home and got the car and followed him. The room downstairs is surrounded by a corridor and a secret room. I stayed there all weekend. The mirrors are all two way mirrors, and Russ has the room wired for sound, so I could see and hear everything. By the way," he turns, pointing a finger at Russ, "you almost went too far with that candle thing. You have no idea how close I was to bursting in on you and slugging you square in the chops."

"Sorry, man. No harm, no foul."

"Miranda, I'm sorry, but I never expected you to say yes, to either the rape or the weekend in the dungeon. I may have set the stage, but honey, you made your own damn bed."

Well, he had me there. My anger slowly begins to subside, then evolves into embarrassment as I recall all of the degrading acts that Nick must have witnessed, and even worse, my reactions to them. Oh God. . . . I'm lucky that he's not the one feeling offended.

The ride home starts out uncomfortably quiet, neither one of us brave enough to break the ice. Lord knows, there is still plenty left unsaid, and once we get started, it has the potential of getting ugly in a hurry. Still, I sneak a look, heartbroken by his stony features. I am sooooo divorced.

"Mad?"

He smiles, in spite of himself, amazed that I'd even have the gumption to ask.

"Mad?.... No.... Hurt?.... maybe. But it's not anything I can't get over. I should have known. You are much too weak to resist the temptations of the flesh, my dear. I should never have put you in that position. I'm just as much to blame. I can't be mad just because it backfired on me. I just wish . . . "

"Wish what?"

"I didn't even think that you were attracted to Russ! What happened to he's a self-centered, egotistical, muscle bound jerk?"

"Uh . . . I think I was a little hasty with that opinion based only on my first impressions. I just never allowed myself to get to know him any better, preferring to stereotype him into a category of men that I have no respect for. I've found that I actually kind of like him."

"Yeah . . . well that is painfully obvious."

Again I wince, my conscience flooding with guilt and shame. Nick drops me off at the house, but doesn't exit the car with me.

"Aren't you coming in?"

"Nah, I think I'll drive around for a little while and do some thinking. This weekend has been just a little too weird for me. I'll be back by bedtime."

*   *   *

I watch dejectedly as Nick drives away. Damn. Don't tell me that I managed to salvage our marriage after a three month separation, only to lose it over a wild and depraved weekend. I wish I could add "meaningless" to the list as well, but it was far from that. Not only did I enjoy and thrive on Russ's control over me, but I also began to see him in another light . . . as a man, a sexy, compelling man, not just as "one of Nick's kinky friends." How is it that I always manage to get myself into these situations? One minute it's okay for me to explore and delve into my fantasies, while the next, it's not. Oh, God, I'm so confused. I need a friend.

Walking into the den, my gaze pauses on my ever faithful buddy, the computer, then settles on the VR suit and swing hanging suggestively nearby. Struggling to resist the urge of drowning my troubles in VR, I activate the computer to jump into the chat rooms hoping to find consolation there. Immediately, the VR software opens, the location icons glowing brightly to tease and tempt me. No, I can't. It may not be safe without Nick there. I haven't even contacted Antonio.

Even though I have several good reasons for not entering the land of make-believe, I hold my breath as I double click on the "Castle of Fantasies" icon. A short description of this Virtual World reveals that I will be entering an old, renovated castle built to satisfy any and all possibly conceived fantasies. The most basic ones can be satisfied immediately, where the more detailed ones need time to become intricately developed. Heck, I don't care. I'm not looking to fulfill a fantasy, just hoping for a little distraction from my current dilemma. Maybe, just maybe, I can even find someone else hanging out in the castle that I can talk to, but that is doubtful considering I haven't pre-arranged anything with Antonio, and only twenty or so people currently have access to these VR worlds. Smiling, I set the timer for one hour and change into my suit, attaching the "sex insert," just in case.

My entrance into the castle isn't nearly as dramatic as my flight onto the yacht. My vision is completely eliminated, leaving me shrouded in a tomb of inky darkness. Soon the black begins to fade into brown, and magically, I find myself standing in a room. It is a small room, constructed completely from stone, yet the comfort from the blazing fire creates a feeling of warmth and familiarity. The only other sights that greet me are first, a sign on a door saying, "Welcome to Castle Fantasy," and second, a bright red, fire alarm pull station. Without hesitation, I pull open the door that leads into the interior of the castle.

The door opens up into a long hallway to my right, and a solid stone wall to my left. The hallway is aligned with brightly glowing torches illuminating the entrances to several other doors, all which appear to be locked. I continue to walk down the corridor, trying each knob as I pass with the same results. Finally, the hallway opens into a huge room, well lit, with another fire burning reassuringly in the corner fireplace. To the right of the fireplace is a beautiful oak, roll-top desk, with a small figure bent over it, so thoroughly engrossed that my presence is not immediately detected.

"Hello!" I call out.

*   *   *

Immediately, the figure stands and turns, poised as if to fight. I continue to walk slowly closer, thrilled to find that I'm not alone, yet not wanting to startle my new-found friend. I get close enough to see that the figure is a woman, and notice her posture immediately begin to relax as she senses my lack of a threat.

"You startled me, Miranda. I thought I was alone."

Her voice is deep and throaty, and very, very seductive. Close enough now to make out her features, I am taken aback by the intensity and beauty of them. She is Oriental with long, straight, shiny, blue-black hair, falling easily to her waist. Her face is perfect, dark brown intelligent eyes, a small pert nose, and a pouty rosebud mouth. Her figure is just as exquisite . . . lean, muscular, controlled. She is wearing only a black, vinyl, bodysuit corset, and a pair of shiny black boots reaching to mid-thigh. She is also casually and fondly stroking the end of a very menacing-looking whip.

"How do you know me?"

"It's my business to know everyone who has access to the program. The real question is, what are you doing here? Antonio did not prepare me properly for your arrival, which causes me to assume that he has no knowledge of it."

"Oh, I'm really sorry. It was a spur of the moment decision. I wasn't aware that I had to let him know in advance. I was just going to explore the castle. I honestly didn't expect to find anyone here."

I stop walking as she begins to move toward me, her stride very determined and calculated. The look on her face is chilling, her eyes hard and cold, yet thoughtful, while her mouth remains in a soft, reassuring smile. Immediately, I know that this is not a woman to challenge. She exudes authority, power and confidence and appears to possess an uncanny ability to read people. I can feel her assessing me, easily summing up my chaotic personality and categorizing it effortlessly, filing it to later analyze and then effectively manipulate. I make my own mental note not to trust or underestimate her, at least not right away. She is dangerous and could be a formidable adversary. Despite my wariness, her smile remains hypnotic, transfixing me as she continues to move in closer, the tall, spiked heels allowing her to look me straight in the eye.

"My name is Raven. I am responsible for running the business aspects of Antonio's VR empire. I guess you can think of me as his secretary/treasurer. Personally, though, I prefer to be referred to as his partner."

Her breath smells sweet as it is blown across my nose for me to inhale. For some reason, I immediately like this woman, knowing that earning her respect will be of utmost importance. I smile back at her, keeping my composure and never losing eye contact.

"Well, Raven. I am very pleased to meet you. Shall I call you Raven, or do you prefer. . . . Mistress?"

Smiling, she takes the flexible end of her whip and places it at the hollow of my throat, then gradually wraps the entire length of the whip around my neck, until there is just a short distance between the handle and my throat. Pulling at the handle, she commands, "Follow me."

Somewhat frightened by the constricting feeling around my neck, I clutch at my throat as she pulls me along.

"Where are you taking me?"

"Just on a mini tour of the castle. I can't have you wandering alone and getting lost, can I?"

Raven guides me back down the same hallway from which I entered, and randomly begins to unlock doors, allowing me a peak inside. Each room is a pre-staged setting based on the most popular and basic fantasies of the human psyche. They are all very elaborate and realistic, almost too realistic.

"Here we have an outdoor cave setting. This is for people, mostly men, who fantasize about living back in the caveman era and enjoy dragging their women around by the hair. It's a very macho fantasy, ready to satisfy the male chauvinist side of any man. Of course, there are also women that request this fantasy, and those are the women that crave a strong man and don't mind being used on that primitive a level."

Raven smiles and then winks at me as she closes the door and leads me over to the next one.

"This here is your classic schoolroom fantasy, and covers areas ranging from a teacher/student fantasy, to finally getting the cheerleader that always turned you down. Of course, if that doesn't apply to the female client, well then, I'm sure there was an elusive football player in her past. We can create the identities of the players to closely match any descriptions given, or if a picture can be provided, that's even better. There are so many possibilities in VR, only limited by one's own imagination."

I find my body tingling as I listen to Raven's alluring voice, momentarily transporting myself into each of the fantasies as she's describing them. Only the impatient tug on my neck snaps me out of my reverie, returning me to the present as we continue on the erotic journey.

She quickly shows me several other basic rooms; a hotel room, a pool hall and bar, a strip club, a gym full of weights and workout equipment, an office, a jail, a library, a doctor's office, you name it. Every imaginable setting is accounted for, even the more difficult ones simulating the outdoors. Raven shows me a deserted island, complete with palm trees and sunshine. The whole concept is so overwhelming that I just gape in awe, suddenly very eager to try one of them out.

"Now this is a fun room," Raven explains, as she unlocks yet another door. She takes me inside and I feel as if I've just stepped into the body of a Boeing 747 airplane. I look down the entire length of the aisle, spotting the cockpit at one end and the restrooms at the other.

"This set also satisfies many fantasies, starting simply at always wanting to pilot a plane, to overcoming a fear of flying, having sex with the stewardess, or meeting an enticing stranger and finally becoming a member of the 'Mile High Club.' We anticipate this to be an extremely popular room once the general public has access. In the meantime, we can fill empty seats with the flip of a switch, immediately crowding the airplane with holograms."

"Wow, this is mind boggling, Raven. How long does it take to set one of these fantasies up?"

"Well, it's always best to give us at least a twenty-four hour notice, but some of the less intricate ones can usually be ready almost immediately, as long as there is at least one other 'real' person available to interact with. Depends on what you're requesting."

"Like, for instance, if I wanted to meet a stranger on this airplane right now, could I do it?"

Raven grins, almost as if she had expected me to ask that. Leading me back into the main room, still controlling my movements by her trusty whip, she forces me to have a seat in a throne-like chair.

"Be a good girl and stay put, and I'll see if there's anybody available to play with right now."

Raven wanders back over to her amazing desk and accesses her computer. In the interim, I make myself comfortable as I analyze the unique chair I find myself occupying. The throne is very strange and appears almost as if it is built for two. Just below where I'm sitting, maybe only an inch lower, is another padded seat, nestled up close to the higher one. There are also distinctive grooves, spread widely apart, for two pair of legs to be cradled in. Also not escaping my notice are several straps conveniently located to helplessly bind someone to this erotic bondage throne. I smile wishfully as I run my hand along the lush red velvet material covering the exquisite chair.

"You're in luck, doll," Raven whispers enticingly into my ear. "I found somebody eager to join you."

I jump, almost falling out of the chair, surprised by her stealthy reappearance.

"Jesus, Raven. You scared me to death."
    Grinning seductively, she replies, "Now we're even."

I cover my heart with my hands, trying to still the erratic beating as Raven takes this opportunity to ask me a few questions.

"Just a couple little details to work out, Miranda. What would you like to be wearing on your flight, or shall I pick out an outfit for you myself?"

Wearing? Geeze, that never occurred to me. What am I wearing right now? I can't believe I hadn't even bothered to check.
    "Um, something sexy of course, easily accessible. What would you wear in the same fantasy, Raven?"
    "I'll take care of you, doll. Have no worries. Sit tight while I work out the details, and then we'll have to wait about fifteen minutes for it to be ready. We can take that time to get to know one another a little better."

* * *

She practically purrs that last sentence, again sending tingles throughout my body. I look down curiously to see what my current outfit consists of noticing that it is nothing special, just a cute little sundress and a pair of comfortable sandals. Hmmmm, must be a "default" outfit for any female guest entering the castle unannounced. Raven returns, positioning herself standing between the widespread legs of the throne. She leans over, looking me suggestively in the eyes.

"All set. Now, whatever shall we do with our time?"

I watch, sucking in my breath, as her hand reaches out, presumably for my breast. Instead, she grins wickedly as she grasps the handle of the whip, somewhat forgotten as it was left to dangle in the comfort of my cleavage. She pulls it out and toward her, dragging me along with it, until my bottom slides off of the upper level of the throne to plop unceremoniously down onto the lower padded seat. Then she proceeds to fasten my legs into the innermost grooves of the chair, seemingly leaving the outer ones for her own legs to nestle into. Once my legs are immobile, she stands facing me once again and pulls on the whip handle until I am looking up at her.

"Do you ever fantasize about making love with another woman, Miranda, or are all the figures in your fantasy world built with a penis?"

"I try to keep my fantasy world open to all possibilities, Raven, completely uninhibited. Some things even carry over into my 'real' world," I answer, thoughtfully . . . breathlessly.

* * *

"Mmmm, good answer. It's not very often that I meet a woman who possesses as much sex appeal as me, Miranda. You have potential, and I find you extremely arousing."

Raven then lowers her head until her lips are within a millimeter of touching my own, and I feel her breath tickle my nose and mouth as she asks, "Would you like for me to kiss you?"

"Yes," I whisper, almost too eagerly.
  "Yes, what?" Raven asks, smiling.
  "Yes, please?"
  "No, try again."

I struggle, trying to decipher what it is that she wants me to say. She still has a grip on the whip handle, and pushes it up between our mouths, seductively licking the side facing her.
  "Lick the handle while you think."

I begin to lick and suck on the other side of the leather device, while searching her eyes for the answer. Raven is careful not to let our tongues co-mingle. Almost immediately, a thought comes to me, and I am almost certain that I now know what she's looking for. I pull my lips away just long enough to say, "Yes, Mistress."

Raven rewards me with a huge smile, and then snakes her tongue around to graze my own before removing the handle completely and covering my mouth with her intoxicating kiss. I melt into the incredible softness of her lips, then yelp as she changes her tactic and starts to nip and bite at me instead. Satisfied, she pulls away and unravels the whip from my throat. Then she climbs up onto the throne to sit behind me.

My back is immediately enveloped in the warmth of her chest, and she playfully kisses the back of my neck as her nose snuggles into the fragrant softness of my hair. Next, I watch as she situates her legs to rest comfortably in the outer grooves of the chair, her legs now even more widely spread than my own. Her arms reach around to clasp me tightly to her body, while her hands work on softly caressing the material of my dress, stimulating my breasts underneath. I can also feel her pubic bone grinding into my lower back and tailbone. Mmmmmm. I relax into her while she continues her slow seduction.

"So tell me, Miranda. Why are you here?"

I try to answer her as best as possible, finding it very difficult to concentrate on speech when all I can do is focus on her roving hands. They are gently caressing my entire torso, awakening all my nerve endings, and then softly touching the tops of my exposed legs. I shiver as she uses her long, manicured nails, and rakes them up the insides of my thighs, stopping at my dampened panties.

"I'm waiting," she demands, impatiently, now stroking and rubbing my crotch expertly while continuing to kiss the back of my neck.

"Ahhhh . . . um . . . my husband, Nick . . . and I had a little . . . confrontation . . . of sorts. He . . . he's off driving . . . to think, so I, I . . . decided to look, ah, for my own . . . distraction. Ohhh, Raven."

"Mmmmm, I see. Nothing like a little sex to take your mind off of your problems, huh?"

"Ah, I think . . . think . . . that's what got, uh, ohhhh . . . got me in this . . . into trouble . . . in the first place."

"Mmmmm, I do recall hearing somewhere that you are quite insatiable. One of these days, you and I will have to play. Are you brave enough to trust me?"

"Why would I need to be brave to. . . . ? OH GOD . . ."

"Don't worry, doll. I'm not going to make you cum. I'm just getting you all worked up for your airplane encounter. It's almost time."

Raven slips one of her tapered nails into my crease and then inserts it deep into my sopping interior. Slowly she pumps it in and out, taking away the clitoral stimulation and any threat of an unintentional climax. The feeling is exquisite, and it is impossible to comprehend that it is not really happening, that I'm actually reclining comfortably in my swing at home. Finally, she removes her finger and asks me to wash it off for her. I take it into my mouth and suck it clean. Then, jumping down from the throne, she releases my legs and announces that it is last call for boarding.

Raven ushers me inside the room, then closes the door behind me. I turn to ask her one more question, only to find that the door is gone, replaced by the interior wall of an airplane. Suddenly panicked, I wonder how on earth I'll be able to get out if I don't like what happens. I scan the interior until I discover the fire alarm, breathing a huge sigh of relief. Ok, ok. Settle down, Miranda.

Next I check to see what interesting outfit Raven has chosen for me. I am wearing tight, shiny black pants that look like they are made from leather, but they're not. They are much lighter, almost that "wet look" fabric. Silently, I thank Raven for selecting the easy access clothing I requested. I should have known that she'd try to make this interesting. I look down to see that I am wearing high, black platform shoes and also a pink, crop-top, angora sweater. It has short sleeves and nestles snuggly against my rib cage, accentuating my breasts to their best advantage.

"May I show you to your seat? I'll just need to have a look at your boarding pass." Startled, I look up to see a very friendly and very attractive stewardess holding her hand out. Is she real? I resist the urge to touch her and wonder where in the heck my ticket is supposed to be. I start to frisk my own pockets, then realize that I have a purse slung over my right shoulder. Praying that Raven has taken care of this little glitch, I open the purse to find the elusive boarding pass. Smiling, I hand it to the patient stewardess.

"First class. Right this way, Miranda."

I start to follow her, becoming immediately aware that the interior of the plane is now a bustle of activity. There are people walking up and down the aisle, tucking away luggage in the overhead storage bins and scouting for extra pillows and blankets. All the same activities you would expect to see on a real flight. Again, it's so hard to convince my brain that this is all a simulation.

*   *   *

The stewardess guides me over to a window seat in the lush and roomy accommodations of the first class section, then reaches behind to close the curtain separating first class from the rest of the airplane. There are a total of twelve seats now remaining in my vision, all currently occupied, all that is, except for the aisle seat directly next to me. I glance at each person, wondering at first if it's a real person or a hologram, and next, if that is the person with whom I'm supposed to have an erotic encounter with. Eager to proceed, I scoot on over into the aisle seat for a closer look.

"I believe that you're in my seat."

"Oh, I apolo. . . . Lucas?!"

"Ah, we meet again, lovely Miranda."

In shock, I slip back on over into my own seat, suddenly uncomfortable that Raven has set me up with Lucas. Hmmmm, this is not what I expected, not what I was hoping for at all. I wanted a stranger. No names, no connections, just a wild "wham, bam, thank you ma'am" encounter.

Lucas sits down and then turns to me saying, "You're not very happy to see me, are you?" Then he reaches a finger across to brush a stray lock of hair away from my face. "What is it about me that you don't like?"

I close my eyes, trying to ignore the electrical charge that radiates throughout my face and scalp from his simple touch. I visualize his sinfully handsome face . . . those incredible teal eyes, the jet black hair, the sun-kissed skin. My God, what's *not* to like? Maybe that's the problem. Maybe I feel inferior, that he has the upper hand . . . that he has the *control.* Ah, not good to not be in control of your own fantasy. Certain that I have pinpointed the reason for my discomfort, I once again open my eyes and focus in on him.

Just as I'm about to answer his question, the captain's voice comes booming over the intercom for all passengers to fasten their safety belts and prepare for takeoff. The stewardess returns and assists Lucas and me with our buckles, then prepares the safety demonstration. I look out the window, amazed to see an airport ramp area, complete with baggage-toting vehicles and line men. Then I actually feel the vibrations of the engine and the airplane start to move as it taxies down the runway. Within minutes, we are airborne. Suddenly playful, I look over at Lucas and smile. "Do *you* have any idea where we are going? I forgot to ask."

He just winks in response and says, "Does it really matter?"

"Guess not." Okay, now what?

"You never answered my question, Miranda. Why don't you like me?"

I look at him thoughtfully, momentarily mesmerized by his incredible eyes, then ask my own question.

"Not many women say 'no' to you, do they?"

"No. But I don't imagine many men turn you away, either. Is that what this is about? You think that I'm a womanizer?"

* * *

I shrug my shoulders and then change the subject. "Do they serve refreshments on this flight? I could use a cocktail."

Lucas shakes his head in amusement. "Sorry, baby. That's one aspect of VR that Antonio hasn't quite perfected, eating and drinking. He can get the texture and flavor to the lips and tongue, but hasn't quite mastered the art of swallowing. Screws up a good blow job, too."

I laugh, and then hesitantly ask Lucas the dreaded question that's been nagging at me since the flight began. "So, what exactly did Raven say to you? I mean, why did you decide to meet up with me here?"

"Oh, Miranda, please. Don't be coy. We both know why I'm here."

Lucas leans closer, whispering lustfully into my ear. "Now, the only thing we have to worry about is *where* you want me to fuck you."

"No! No! Oh my God, Lucas. It's not supposed to be like this. It's supposed to be ... spontaneous, not planned."

"Nothing's planned, baby. It's like we've just met and felt an immediate attraction to one another. And now you are playing the indignant female pretending to be insulted by my blatant invitation, when what you'd really like to do is tear my clothes off and have your way with me. Suit yourself."

"That's it. I'm not going to sit here and listen to you puff your feathers. Please excuse me."

I stand up, destination unknown, but determined that I will no longer subject myself to his arrogance. As I pass by him and out into the isle, Lucas reaches up and grabs my ass, the final straw. I turn around, furious at his nerve, and slap him soundly across his smug face. "Go fuck yourself, you self-centered ass." Extremely pleased that I did not allow him to get away with manhandling me, I strut down the isle until I spy an unoccupied restroom and seek temporary refuge within. Just as I'm about to slide the lock in place, the door comes bursting open, throwing me backwards and onto the closed toilet lid.

"What the . . . ?"

Lucas barges in, even more incensed over my slap than I was about his unwanted groping. Oh God. I'm so dead. Slamming and locking the door behind him, he quickly turns to me, appearing absolutely livid, obviously struggling to get his anger under control.

Pointing a threatening finger at me, he utters through clenched teeth, "Don't you *ever* slap me again. EVER!"

I cringe and scoot back, certain that he's going to rip my head off, but instead, he just stands next to the door, continuing to breathe erratically.

"Get up!"
  "Wha . . . what? Why?"
  "I said, stand the fuck up . . . now!"

Terrified, I jump to my feet, and start to try and calm him down.

"I'm sorry, Lucas. I don't know what came over me. I . . ."

My words are cut short as he grabs hold of my hair and pulls me smack into his chest, kissing me viciously, bruising my mouth. Immediately, every thought and every feeling disappears except for intense lust and passion . . . and . . . need. Greedily, I kiss him back, not at all intimidated by the punishing kiss. Starting deep within the pit of my belly, I feel liquid heat rapidly spread through my veins, setting my entire body on fire. I feel animal, primitive and can focus on nothing but Lucas's presence. My God. I want to fuck him. I want to fuck him hard. I want to fuck him fast. I want to scream.

With disgust, Lucas pushes me from him so that I'm standing just in front of the toilet again. The desire and lust clearly visible in his eyes is scary, yet excites me. We stare at each other, unable to catch our breath, quickly becoming lightheaded as we fill the small cabin with carbon monoxide. Lucas takes the back of his hand and swipes it across his lips, as if to remove the memory of my kiss, and becomes even more angry when the simple gesture only heightens his arousal.

"Take off your pants."

I meet his gaze, rising to his challenge, and begin to remove my pants slowly, my eyes never leaving his. No way am I going to allow him to reduce me to a cowering, pathetic, whimpering frightened schoolgirl. He wants a fight, well he's going to get a fight. Finally, I wriggle the pants down from my hips until they fall into a heap around my ankles. I try to step out of them, but cannot get beyond the barrier provided by the clunky shoes. Beaten, I just stand there and wait for his next move, eyes still locked with his, daring him.

"All the way."

"I . . . can't . . . get . . . them . . . past . . . my . . . shoes," I practically spit out through clenched teeth.

Lucas walks over to me, my bravado slipping momentarily as he takes hold of my thong panties. In one powerful jerk, he rips them from my body, causing me to gasp in surprise. The act is almost painful, yet the excitement immediately following, overshadows, then suffocates any physical hurt I felt initially. All it serves to do is reinforce my desire not to cringe before him, and issue my own unspoken challenge. Is that all you've got, fucker?

Lucas grabs my hair again and pulls backward until I cry out.

"I said, take off your pants, not pull them down. I meant it. Now, do what you have to do, but get them off. I am running out of patience with you."

I am pushed back into a sitting position as Lucas releases his hold on my hair, finding myself once again warming the lid of the pot. Never have I ever felt such murderous thoughts, the urge to fling myself at him and scratch his eyes out very hard to ignore. Luckily, I manage to stifle them as I work on first removing my shoes, then my pants. After kicking them aside, I stand proudly, only to witness Lucas in the process of hurriedly removing his own constricting clothing.

In no time at all, Lucas is completely nude, and I am held utterly spellbound. He is beautiful, muscular, built quite similarly to Russ, only darker, and shiny with sweat. Somehow, seeing his body covered with perspiration makes him only more desirable, irresistible, magnetic. And his cock is magnificent . . . rigidly standing out, straining against the confines of its own skin, deepening to an angry purple. I can't help but imagine it thrusting aggressively into me, practically collapsing against my weakened knees at the thought. Oh my God. I could cum just thinking about it. Lucas's next command saves me from embarrassing myself any further.

"Now your shirt."

Ready, wanting nothing more than to wildly fuck this man, I pull the sweater up and over my head, and quickly remove the satin bra hidden underneath. Standing as gloriously naked as he, I watch as he repositions himself in the cramped quarters. He leans against the wall opposite the sink and then slowly lowers himself until his bare feet are braced against the foot of the sink, then turns to look at me.

"Ride it, bitch."

I smile and straddle him seductively, positioning myself just above his throbbing member.

"Gladly," I whisper back, as I let my full weight fall and envelope him in one fell swoop.

*   *   *

Two distinctly different sounds are wrenched from us, his an animalistic groan, mine a scream of intense pleasure combined with a sigh. Lucas grabs hold of my hips and then prepares to take me on the ride of my life, repeatedly lifting me up, then slamming me back down the full length of his ultimately aroused cock. Each thrust is overwhelming, ears tingling while my eyes fill with unshed tears of pure ecstasy. Just when I think I can take no more of the punishing encounter, Lucas drives home one more time then releases himself inside me, flooding me with several spurts of his thick, creamy cum and marking me with his own individualized masculine scent. Seconds behind him, I too get caught up in the throes of my own orgasm, collapsing and falling across his chest. Breathlessly, I open my mouth to speak, but never have the opportunity to utter the words. Magically, I am transported back into my basement as my hour comes to a close, the preset timer impeccably reliable.

CHAPTER 8

■

CONFRONTATIONS

Monday morning comes much too quickly as I swat at the snooze button somewhat annoyed. Oh God, I don't want to go to work today, with the events of the weekend still plaguing me. Well, at least Nick decided to come home last night. That's a good sign, I guess. I had already gone to bed, quite depressed and loaded, opting to drown my sorrows with wine after the VR experience failed to lighten my mood. If anything, I was even more confused after my confrontation with Lucas. I have to admit, it was quite thrilling. He must have gotten so pissed when I just disappeared after the timer went off. Well, at least he "got off" before that happened. Two minutes earlier and we would have both been left extremely frustrated. I might have had to go back in a second time. As it was, Lucas probably expected me to reappear, irking him further when I didn't.

Moaning, I turn to look at Nick who has just begun to stir. "Morning, hon."

Groaning, he replies, "Already? Feels like I just fell asleep."

"Well, maybe you did. When did you get home last night?"

"Mmmmm, right around midnight, I think."

"Ah, you've had plenty of sleep, but I think I'm going to blow off going to work today. I'm seriously hung over."

"Well, unfortunately, I don't have that luxury. I have to go in. A world run by computers has no tolerance or compassion for their human counterparts. They'll crash, despite how much sleep I've had. Now, Lois, hand me my cape."

Giggling, I reach out my hand and lovingly stroke Nick's face. "We're okay?"

"Yeah, baby, we're okay."

Nick pulls me over to him and kisses me leisurely, gently, thoroughly. Then he flops me over so that my back is cradled against his stomach, both of us resting on our right sides. Slowly, he enters me, tenderly melting away the ice crystals that had begun to form around my heart in self-preservation. Ah, the coupling is sweet, magical, healing, and both Nick and I feel quite back to normal when it's over. With one final kiss to the tip of my nose, Nick hops out of bed and into the shower. I quickly call work and leave a message for Beau telling him that I am not feeling well enough to join him at the office today, then fall back into a blissful sleep.

When next I awaken, it's just after 10 AM, and I'm feeling wonderfully refreshed. Headache and hangover gone, I quickly decide that I am quite capable of putting in a few hours at Handymans after all. No sense wasting all this newfound energy just sitting around the house. By 11:30 AM, I am out the door and whistling my way to work.

The lobby is lifeless when I enter, not a soul in sight. Even Wesley has made himself scarce, almost as if Mr. Miller had given everyone the day off in my absence. Checking my appointment book, I realize that today is solidly booked for the guys, and that they are all probably out on calls. Feeling somewhat guilty for the bind I left Beau in, and on such a busy day, I quickly brew a fresh pot of coffee and then take him a cup.

The door to his office is closed, and I hesitate just long enough before knocking to identify a very feminine squeal coming from within. Pausing, I strain to listen more closely, almost certain that he is sexually "entertaining" a lady friend. The bastard! All this time he led me to believe that he remains celibate, that he is too offensive for women to find sexually attractive. He even had me feeling so sorry for him, that I dressed kinky and masturbated to appease his voyeuristic fantasies. I can't believe he had me so fooled! And, and, if he's not really disfigured, not really unattractive, why doesn't he want me? There were times when I begged him to take me, to fuck me, to use me, but never once did he seem interested in anything but watching. What does "she" have that I don't have?

Confused by the irrational feelings flooding my emotions, I move away and race back to my desk, trying to come to grips with my hurt. I feel so naive, knowing now that's he's been using me, *toying* with me, probably even laughing at me. How could he do that to me? All I ever wanted was to help him with his burden. I didn't deserve this.

Reaching blindly into my purse, I yank out my stash of tissues and start dabbing at my eyes, hoping to quickly quell the flow of my tears. Then, of course, I try to rationalize. Why do I care? I have a husband I adore who allows me to pursue any and all fantasies I feel comfortable going after. I have a virtual world to explore all the ones I'm not so at ease with. Why does it bother me so to discover that Mr. Miller has no sexual interest in me? "It's not that, Miranda, it's the fact that he made a fool out of you. That's what's really upsetting you. Don't be hurt. Don't get mad. Get even," persuades the tiny voice inside.

Sniffling, my tears subsiding as my anger increases, I start to stuff the remaining tissues back into my purse when my fingers close around a hard, cool object. Smiling again, I lift the bottle out and hold it up as I begin to create my own form of revenge. Ah, Russ's herbs, the aphrodisiac herbs. I had almost completely forgotten about them, thoughtlessly tossing them into my purse as my sweatshirt unceremoniously joined the neglected piles of laundry on the basement floor. Oh, I couldn't think of a more perfect way to get back at him.

Grinning now, I begin to stir a small amount of the herbs into Beau's cup of coffee, until no trace of them remain, then meander back to his office door. Boldly, I knock on the door and then twist the knob, surprised when it swings wide open. Pretending not to suspect anything amiss, I begin to address Mr. Miller.

"Good morning, Beau. Sorry I'm late. I woke up feeling terrible this morning, but after a few more hours rest, I felt like a whole new person. I decided to surprise you with a fresh cup of coffee and the promise of at least a half a day's work."

The silence behind the curtain, as well as the lack of movement, is almost comical as I wait for a response. Finally, Beau clears his throat.

"Ah, Miranda. What a . . . a nice surprise. Of course I'm glad that you could make it after all. Um, you can just set the coffee down on the edge of my desk and I'll get to it in just a moment. I'm in the middle of something rather critical, unfortunately demanding my full attention."

I bet it does. I place the coffee on the desk as requested, but rather than take the cue and leave, I close the door and have a seat in the chair opposite his desk.

"Oh, come on, Beau. I've had the most incredible, wild weekend I've ever had. You just have to let me tell you all about it while you drink up. I'm just bursting, and I know you'll get a kick out of it."

With all of his blood rushed to the "other head," Beau is unable to come up with a plausible excuse quickly enough to make me leave, and succumbs gracefully. Again, I have to stifle a giggle as I watch his finger slip up under the curtain and begin to drag the coffee cup toward him.

"By all means, then, Miranda, please, enlighten me regarding your weekend activities."

I spend the next fifteen minutes describing my encounter after work on Friday night. Beau apologizes for keeping me so late, convinced that it was his fault that I landed in the predicament I had. I explained to him that I eventually ended up enjoying it thoroughly, and that he shouldn't blame himself. After a slight pause in my story, his empty coffee cup is slid back to the edge of his desk.

"We need to invest in a different brand of coffee. That cup tasted pretty stale."

"No problem. I'll take care of that this afternoon."

For the next fifteen minutes, I explain how Russ convinced me into agreeing to spend the weekend in his dungeon and all the fine tortures that I exposed myself to as a result. Beau is pretty quiet for most of the verbal dissertation, then out of the blue, gets on the intercom.

"Dante, I need you in my office immediately."

"Yes, sir."

In less than twenty seconds, "Dante" is knocking on the office door and Beau invites him in. Oh my God. I hope I didn't just get him into trouble. That certainly wasn't my intent.

* * *

He walks in, a bit surprised to see me, then asks, "What's wrong? Your page sounded urgent."

"Please close the door and then block it. I don't want Miranda to be able to leave."

Russ and I look at one another, completely befuddled. What the hell is going on?

"Beau?" I venture. "I don't understand."

Beau's voice sounds positively icy when he finally speaks. "What was in the coffee, Miranda?"

Oh my God, so busted.

"Uh, just a little cream and sugar. Why?"

The sound of his fist slamming into his desk causes both Russ and I to jump simultaneously.

"Don't screw with me, Miranda. I've got a raging hard-on right now that I can't account for. My veins feel like they've got lava flowing through them, and I have an uncontrollable urge to fuck my chia-pet. What was in the God-damn coffee!"

I wince at the full-blown rage I hear in his voice, then reel backwards even more as Russ joins in and double teams me.

"You bitch! You stole them, didn't you? I've been looking all over for them. I can't believe you just up and took them!"

"What? What'd she take? Did she poison me? For God's sake, tell me what I just drank!"

"Calm down. Just some herbs. You're not going to die. You're just going to be insatiably horny for the next eight hours or so."

Oh my. I am soooo backed into a corner. What am I going to do? Well, denying it seems pointless, plus I'm sure the expression on my face has already given me away. With no other option available, I extend my claws and get ready for battle.

"Well . . . Beau. . . . if you hadn't been back there fucking some floozy when I got to work, I never would have used them on you. And you," I screech, as I turn to face Russ, "had no right to use those herbs on me in the first place. Serves you right, you cock-sucking bastard!"

Russ looks momentarily shocked by my vulgar misuse of the English language, while Beau mellows out some, probably a little embarrassed over getting caught.

"I apologize for my little indiscretion, but that didn't give you the right to drug me. Where are the herbs now?"

"None of your damn business."

For the next several moments, a lot of shuffling about and whispering goes on behind Mr. Miller's curtain. Then finally, a creamy chocolate leg appears, soon followed by the rest of an extremely exotic female body. From behind the curtain steps a very tall, very regal, and very beautiful black woman. Her gaze immediately settles on me, then narrows, accusingly. Her hair is long and bound in corn rows, exquisitely decorated with colorful designer beads. Her skin is creamy and flawless, accentuated by a short, bright yellow leather dress and a pair of yellow heels. She continues to stare at me, as if waiting.

"I'll ask you one more time. Where are the herbs?"

Before I can answer, Russ interjects. "They've got to be here somewhere, or she wouldn't have been able to use them on you. They're probably in her purse or something. Maybe on her desk somewhere."

"Ah, I bet you're right, Russ. Janelle, my sweet, would you mind searching Miranda's personal belongings and around her desk for them?"

"Not at all, love."

She has an English accent! Not at all what I would have expected her voice to sound like.

"Russ, what do they look like?"

"Well, they should be in a small brown glass bottle."

"Janelle, if you should find them, please bring them back here to me. Oh, and would you mind getting me another cup of coffee?"

"Consider it done."

Gracefully, she confiscates the empty cup and exits the office. In less than five minutes, she returns, a shiny brown bottle in her grasp, as well as another cup of fresh coffee.

"Thank you darling. Please give those to Russ and have a seat next to Miranda. Russ, I want you to mix up a very potent amount of those herbs into that coffee and then supervise Miranda as she drinks it."

"What if she won't drink it? What if she spits it out at me?"

"Oh, she'll drink it, because if she doesn't, we'll take her out into the parking lot and force feed it to her, enema style."

Russ grins from ear to ear, I'm sure visualizing me draped over the hood of a car while the warm coffee is pumped slowly into my unwilling ass.

"I'll drink it, I'll drink it! No need to resort to violence, but why? Why do you want me horny? I mean . . ."

"You mean, you're always horny, so why do I feel the need to increase your sex drive?" Beau asks, maliciously. "I'll tell you why. Because, if I'm going to suffer through the afternoon in this state, so are you, baby."

"Ah, so maybe now, you'll want to fuck me."

"What?! Jesus Christ, Miranda. Is that why you did this? Because you wanted me to fuck you?! I can't believe this."

Russ hands me the drugged coffee, and I reluctantly sip it while I give Beau the rest of my explanation.

"For weeks, you've led me to believe that you were incapable of sex, always thwarting any advance or invitation I made in your direction. I thought it was because of your 'condition,' whatever that's supposed to be. And then I find you here . . . with her, obviously quite capable of pleasing a woman. I was hurt that you never thought of me in that way, and were probably laughing at my lame attempts at seducing you. This was the perfect way to get back at you. Give you the herbs, get you so incredibly horny that you'd stoop so low as to even fuck me, and then I'd turn *you* down."

Beau can't resist chuckling, despite the feeling of betrayal. "Miranda, Janelle is not a married woman. You are. I make it a point not to mess with married women. I wouldn't like having to look over my shoulders all the time wondering if there is an enraged husband following me, ready to strike me down. Resisting you has been the greatest challenge of my lifetime. As it is, I've let things get too far, but I had to have something. Watching you, listening to you recap your sexual adventures are all at once heaven and hell. God, I thought you knew that."

I finish the last sip of my coffee wondering how on Earth I managed to once again misinterpret a situation, therefore creating an even worse one. Will I never learn? What is wrong with me?

"Oh God, Beau. I'm so sorry. Please don't hate me."

"I don't hate you, Miranda, but you win. There's no way I can deny my desire for you under these conditions. I'm *going* to fuck you. And then I'm going to fuck you again. And again, and again, and again. For a solid eight hours, or until this drug wears off, I'm going to pound into your treacherous little body. I'm going to make you scream. I'm going to make you beg. I'm going to make you cry. I'm going to make you sigh. I'm. . . . going . . . to. . . . make . . . *you*! Be careful what you wish for, Miranda. It just might come true. Russ, can you get the blindfold out of my bottom file drawer? I think it only appropriate that since she stole from you, you should be the one responsible for taking away her sense of sight."

"Ah, let the games begin." Russ announces, much too enthusiastically.

"I also have some silk scarves in that drawer. Use them to tie Miranda's hands behind her back."

"You're the boss."

Russ takes his time placing the blindfold over my eyes and securing it in place, eliminating any chance that it will slip and reward me with any insight into what's in store for me. Next he binds my hands behind my back, using a scarf not only at my wrists, but another at my elbows as well. By now, the aphrodisiac has already entered my bloodstream and is beginning to wreak some havoc with my mind, raising my body temperature several degrees as well as heightening the rest of my senses. My breathing quickens as my anticipation intensifies, my body eager to live up to the challenge of nonstop sex. Please . . . hurry.

The wait is interminable, and the three of them are exceptionally quiet, hardly making a sound. Just when I think they're going to leave me standing there, I begin to feel hands touching several parts of my body concurrently. One pair of hands is working on the buttons of my blouse, another is removing my shoes and thigh highs, while the last pair is working on the zipper of my skirt. Someone is kissing my lips, but I can't tell who. The lips are soft, so I assume they're Janelle's. I also feel lips on the inside of my thigh, and more kisses being pressed into the small of my back Oh God, I'm in heaven.

Soon my blouse and bra are unclasped and pulled back over my shoulders to drape across my bound arms. The person behind me begins to wind the excess material around the silk scarves, utilizing my own clothing for further bondage purposes. My skirt and panties quickly follow the removal of my stockings and shoes, until I am left standing completely naked. Then the true assault begins. Lips, fingers, hands, tongues, mouths . . . all licking and sucking and biting and touching and groping and probing and pinching. At one point, I have mouths and tongues lapping away at my pussy, ass and nipples all at the same time. Lost in glorious bliss, I succumb to the first of many orgasms I'm certain to experience this afternoon.

Next I find myself being pushed to my knees, then encouraged to sit on a waiting face. Immediately, an eager tongue begins to clean up the mess from my climax, while a persistent cock coaxes my mouth open and commences to thoroughly use it. Back and forth it glides, in and out, hitting the back of my throat on one stroke, then dueling with the tip of my tongue on the next. Not to be left out, the person behind me, now also on his knees, takes the bottom half of my hair, being careful not to upset the blindfold, and wraps it around his cock. Once it is completely surrounded by my silky tresses, he begins to masturbate, using my hair as a form of lubrication. Luckily for me, the two men have their rhythm in sync, one pulling in one direction while the other pushes in the opposite.

We maintain this position until the man behind me spews his seed into my hair just as Janelle beneath me brings about my second orgasm. The man currently ravaging my mouth quickly removes his still throbbing cock, and then pushes me over forward, until my face is smashed into Janelle's crotch, her delectable feminine scent taunting me.

Unable to brace myself with my arms, she is forced to accept the full brunt of my weight, but her squeals indicate that she's not too terribly upset. I begin to lick and suck at her, praying that they don't let me suffocate in the process, while I feel someone entering my upraised pussy from behind. Oh God.

The thrusting is relentless, powerful, potent, exquisite. I am unable to shout out my ecstasy as my face remains buried in the juices of Janelle, however, the man who made the mess in my hair is now alternating between pinching my nipples and pulling back on my head so that I can catch an occasional breath. Still, nobody says a thing, as if the entire encounter had been previously choreographed and practiced to perfection. Everybody just *knows* what they are supposed to do, myself included. Finally, the man behind me groans out his release, flooding me with his sperm, then changes places with whoever is tormenting my nipples.

Again, I feel myself being entered from behind, only much more slowly, calculating. He is swirling his cock around, almost as if trying to completely cover it in the mixture of my and the other man's cum. Then he withdraws, and the light comes on. It has to be Russ, and he's going for my ass. My anal violation is momentarily delayed as Janelle finally lets herself go and climaxes, squirting her fragrant nectar all over my face. Beau pulls my head back in the nick of time, saving me from an imminent drowning, obviously familiar with her sexual responses. I gasp for air, then suddenly gasp for another reason all together, as Russ begins to enter my ass and fuck it as relentlessly as he had in his dungeon.

Janelle squeezes her thighs tightly together, allowing my head a resting place while Russ continues to plunge into my ass. Somebody's fingers begin to tease and tantalize my clit, while another finger slides unobstructed into my pussy. I never knew it could feel like this. I don't want it to ever end.

But end it does. Janelle is the first to speak up that she'd love to stick around, but that she has a previous engagement that she can't ignore. Russ also had to bow out, sheepishly stating that unfortunately, he hadn't consumed any of the drug and is out of commission for a while. Somehow, I don't think that Beau is overly upset, probably relishing in the knowledge that he can finally make good on his earlier threats.

Somebody helps me to stand so that Janelle can get up off the floor and get herself together. Soon the office door closes for the last time, leaving me solely at the mercy of Beau's imagination and his artificially increased sex drive. Still, the thought is arousing to me, that I'm finally going to be ravaged by my mysterious boss. Who is he? To know him, yet not know him at all, only intensifies this cat and mouse game. What's he doing right now? How close is he standing to me? Is that his breath I'm feeling on my shoulder? What's he thinking?

I stand waiting, afraid to even move a muscle, then hear him sit in the chair directly behind me. Grasping my hips, he pulls me stumbling backwards until my legs are straddling his, then eases me downward. Oh, yes, right onto a magnificent cock. The cock that will no doubt ease the fire raging out of control within. He steadies and controls my movements, lifting me up, pulling me down . . . sometimes slowly, other times maniacally. Once, he even holds me up, poised at the tip of his cock, and just waits. I begin to wriggle, trying to squirm my way down, but he doesn't let me. It's not until I beg and grovel and promise him unconditional devotion that I'm finally allowed to slide back down and lose myself in the splendor of his rigid thickness. We both climax again, but the release doesn't even begin to assuage the burning desire and ache we feel coursing through our bodies. Again and again we fuck, against the wall, arched backwards across his desk, draped over the back of a chair, on the floor, on his lap, to finally end under a torrid stream of hot water from his bathroom shower. Several hours have gone by, and I know that Nick must be sick with worry, not even aware that I changed my mind and went to work today. Oh, God, how am I going to explain this one to him?

Beau unties my hands and then exits the bathroom before I have a chance to remove my blindfold. Damn, I was so close. I finish the shower and delighted, spot some fresh clothing on the counter. Not what I arrived in, but at least they are warm, comfy and dry. As I walk back into Beau's office, I can't help but notice the disarray. Furniture knocked over, clothing scattered about ... mostly mine, I come to determine, and office supplies strewn in all directions, obviously disturbed by the wild coupling on top of his desk. I pause in front of his curtain, sure that he's sitting behind it.

"Now what?" I ask, hesitantly. "Do you need my resignation?"

"I'd have to say that my trust has been somewhat shattered. It'll be a while before I can accept a cup of coffee that you've prepared."

"It's probably best if I just gather my things and we go our separate ways. Everything's different now. The office is set up and running smoothly. If you hire someone right away, there shouldn't be any repercussions."

"Goodnight, Miranda."

"Goodbye, Beau."

I gather up my meager belongings quickly and head out the door, halfway home before I realize that I left my purse behind. Damn it. That's what I get for being in such a hurry. Nick is going to be so upset when I finally get home. It's already dark, probably after 9 PM. I turn around and start heading back to the office, thankful that I at least have the keys to the door on my person.

The building is completely dark and empty upon my return. As I enter, I have the uneasy feeling that I'm trespassing, and that I'm under heavy surveillance.

Don't be ridiculous, Miranda. You have a perfectly valid reason for being here.

I find my purse and start to head back to the lobby door, when my inquisitiveness gets the better of me. This may be my one and only chance at ever finding out what's behind Mr. Miller's curtain. I may not learn anything more about him, but at least my curiosity will be satisfied. Against my better judgement, I head in the direction of Beau's office.

I try the handle, expecting to find it locked, then smile in surprise as it opens effortlessly. The office is dark and vacated, no sign that Beau is anywhere nearby. Cringing somewhat, I flip on the light switch then hold my breath, expecting bells and whistles to notify all of my intrusion. When nothing happens, I step inside and shut the door behind me. Eagerly, I head for the curtain.

What I find is astonishing, a veritable control panel of switches and monitors. I feel like I'm behind the security guard's desk at Fort Knox or something. Anxious to see what all the switches are responsible for, I seat myself in the comfortable chair, still warm from Beau's backside. I begin flipping levers and buttons, watching in amazement as the monitors come to life. Beau has cameras placed all over this building, and I play with the one located in the lobby, zooming in on my very own desk, or what used to be my desk. Man, this thing is so powerful, one could easily see straight down my blouse from this angle. Another monitor shows his dark and empty bathroom, just slightly illuminated by the light seeping in from his office. Two more monitors show additional offices, but it's too dark to be able to ascertain which ones.

With another flip of a toggle, all four monitors momentarily go dark, then begin to light up slowly. Curiously, I watch as four new rooms come into sight, then open my mouth in bewilderment as I recognize the rooms. Oh my God. These cameras are in my *house!!* I can clearly identify my bedroom, my bathroom, my kitchen and the computer area of my basement. How can this be? Who is Mr. Miller, and how did he get into my house to install hidden cameras? Oh my God, am I in danger? Is Nick in danger?

Just as this thought passes through my confused brain, I see Nick come into view on the kitchen monitor. He has his coat on, as if he just got home. Oh, no. He's been out looking for me, I'm sure of it. I have to call him. I look down searching for the phone, only to notice that there are two phones sitting side by side on his techno console. One looks just like the phone at my desk, with several different incoming and outgoing lines, and the other is a red, superhero phone, just like the one in all the Batman movies. Totally befuddled, I pick up the familiar phone and quickly dial my home number.

I watch Nick's head turn in the direction of the phone as it rings, jumping when the "bat phone" also starts ringing. Knowing that I'm taking an awfully big risk, I answer it and hold it up to my ear, hearing nothing but heavy breathing. Oh God. He knows. He knows that I'm here.

"Hello?"

I screech and then drop both phones as my own voice rings loud and clear through the ear piece of the "bat phone." I just called myself! I dialed my home number and it rang in here. What in heaven's name is going on? I hang up both phones and continue to watch Nick as a very unpleasant concept crosses my mind. No, it couldn't be. Could it? Nick, Mr. Miller? No . . .

Nick picks up the phone and begins pressing buttons, then hangs it back up again with a thoughtful expression. Oh, please, don't let it be so. The more I think about the possibility, the more it makes sense. No wonder he has never let me see him. But what about his voice? Beau and Nick sound nothing alike. I search the control panel looking for some more clues, and find them. Sure enough, there is a microphone protruding from the console. I lean forward and speak into it. Nothing happens. I look around until I find an on/off switch, and try again. My world quickly begins to crumble as I hear my words broadcast out into the office, cleverly disguised. Oh, the bastard.

Still suspecting, but not yet positive, I decide to try out one more test. Picking up the phone a the second time, I again dial my home number. This time it rings at the house, but not in the office. Nick answers the phone, the call forwarding obviously deactivated.

"Hello."

"Hi, baby." I respond, with higher spirits than I actually feel.

"Miranda! Where are you, honey? I've been worried to death."

I bet you have.

"I felt better after my little nap this morning and decided to come into the office after all. Beau had tons of work for me to do, so I stayed until it was all done."

Nick casually asks, "Oh, so are you still at the office?"

"Yes. I was halfway home and then realized I had forgotten my purse, so I came back for it. I should be home pretty soon."

I watch Nick look directly into the camera, then move toward it as he says, "Okay, baby. I'll be waiting for you." Next, his hand comes up and the screen goes black.

"See you soon."

Oh, I can't believe it, but the proof is right there in front of me as I follow him from room to room, systematically disabling all four of the cameras. He *is* Mr. Miller! How could I not have known about his double life? And why all of this? Just to spy on me? Does he trust me so little that he has to know my every move? Is he afraid and trying to protect me? And from what, myself? How long has this been going on, since my return home?

I begin to feel nauseated as everything comes together with stunning clarity. My own husband, obsessed. Just like Russ had been, maybe still is. Russ . . . he has to know the truth. Those two have been in cahoots since the start. God damn, do I feel duped. What am I going to do?

Nothing, Miranda. You're going to go home and act like nothing is wrong. Then tomorrow, you're going to have the house re-keyed!

Reluctantly, I listen to the voice of reason . . . or is it?

CHAPTER 9

■

REALIZATIONS

Pretending not to know is very difficult, especially when all I want to do is shake Nick and ask him, "why?" As soon as he leaves for the office, I quickly call the locksmith and request that all my locks be changed. He informs me that he can be here in an hour. Nervously, I chomp on my nails. What am I doing? I can't just lock him out of his own home, keep him from his things. Eventually I'm going to have to face him. Eventually, but not now. He can just stay at a motel for a few days, buy some new clothes to get by on, a new toothbrush. I'll call him at the office as soon as we have new locks and tell him that I don't want to see him for a few days, maybe ever again. God, it's still so inconceivable that Nick could deceive me so thoroughly.

With time to kill, I sit down at the computer and e-mail both Angela and Antonio that I'd like to hook back up with them again in VR, preferably around noon today at the Castle. Then, I sit back and watch as the locksmith does his thing. It is almost noon when he leaves, assuring me that no one can enter uninvited, providing me with both sets of keys. I thank him as I usher him out the door, anxious to barricade myself within. Convinced that all the locks are bolted and secure, I race to the basement to make the fated phone call. As luck would have it, he doesn't answer, and I am routed to the voice mail box of "Beau Miller."

"Hello, Beau, or should I say . . . Nick? Your secret is out. I know who you are, and I know what you've been doing. I am so disgusted, that I can't even face you right now. All the locks have been changed at the house, so don't even try to contact me for the next several days. I can't believe that you would stoop to something this low, Nick. I'll contact you when I feel that we can talk about this. Goodbye."

The ache in my heart as I hang up the phone is suffocating. I can barely breathe. It is with tears in my eyes that I read Angela's reply that she and Antonio will gladly meet me at the Castle at noon. Checking the time, I realize that I'm already late. Quickly, I don the suit and insert, click on the Castle icon, then fasten the helmet to my head as I situate myself comfortably in the swing. Then, with the turn of a knob, I'm standing in the foyer of the Castle.

Angela and Antonio aren't there waiting for me, so I enter the castle and head in the direction of Raven's desk, and what I assume to be, the reception area. Raven greets me with a cat-like smile, then invites me to sit on a stunning leather couch while I wait for the others.

*   *   *

"How've you been, doll? You don't look very happy."

"I'm not. Things have gone from bad to worse with my husband. I'm afraid it may be over for good."

"Aw, sweetie, I'm sorry. That's too bad. I know he means the world to you."

Raven tries to comfort me, stroking my forehead and whispering soothing and encouraging words, but I remain pouting miserably. Finally, I see Antonio and Angela entering hand in hand, and can't help but shiver at Antonio's image. He looks just like Lucas, and Lucas gives me the creeps. Joyous to see Angela, however, I jump up and race to greet her.

"Oh, I've missed you so much." I exclaim, as I squeeze her in an incapacitating hug.

"Well, I guess so." She laughs, when she is able to catch her breath. "Guess what, Randi? I have the best news!"

"What?" I ask, excitedly, my mood already beginning to lighten.

"Antonio and I are getting married in June. I want you to be my Matron of Honor."

"Oh my God, you guys! That's wonderful! Of course I'll be your Matron of Honor! Uh, just one quick question, though."

"Yes?"

"Have you guys actually met in person yet, or is this going to be a 'virtual wedding'?"

Both Angela and Antonio start bursting out laughing, then finally get a hold of themselves.

*   *   *

"Of course we've met. We've actually been living together for the past month. Guess I haven't kept you up to date. It happened so fast that even I'm having trouble keeping up."

"Well, I'm so happy for you, and even happier to be a part of it."

Antonio must have sensed my reluctance to speak intimately with Angela in his presence, and chivalrously offers to excuse himself so that we can talk freely. Then Raven offers us the use of any room that strikes our fancy to become reacquainted in. Without hesitation, we both immediately request the "strip club" location and then laugh over our respective sentimentality. Raven smiles knowingly, then leads us into the room to have a seat. She warns us that it will take approximately ten minutes for any type of atmosphere to be incorporated, but to be patient. Angela and I scarcely notice, so wrapped up in our own conversation.

Before long we are chatting again like the old friends we are, and I heartbreakingly tell her about my situation with Nick. She is disappointed, knowing all that we've gone through to stay together, and offers me some sound advice.

"Randi, you've got to give him a chance to explain. Maybe there's something you don't know. Look at all the things he's overlooked and forgiven you for. Even if he has no excuse, and just temporarily lost his mind, it's not anything worse than what you've done. But you shouldn't just push him away. Let him come home and discuss it with him. I would love to discover that Antonio loves me so much that he may lose his mind a time or two and do something crazy like that."

"Yeah, I suppose you're right, Angela. But where do you draw the line between love and obsession? Are they one and the same?"

"Good question. I know you don't need to be in love to be obsessed, but do you become obsessed if you are truly in love? Hmmmm, definitely a point to think about. You and Nick have both done some awfully crazy things in the name of love. I think you're both a little obsessed with one another."

"Oh, Angela. I knew you were the right person to come to about this. How did you become so wise?"

Smiling, she pats my hand in understanding, then gets up quickly. "Oh, shoot. I have to use the little ladies' room, but I don't know if that's possible in VR! I may have to exit the program and then come back in. Wait for me here, Randi. I'll be back in a flash. Mr. Swivel Hips up there can keep you company while I'm gone."

I glance up to see a very handsome male dancer gyrating on the stage, slowly removing what's left of his skimpy costume. Geeze, how long has he been up there, and how could I not have noticed? Happy with the distraction, I sit back and continue to watch the show as Angela hurriedly leaves the room.

Within five minutes, Antonio is poking his head in the door and crooking a finger at me to follow him. Sighing to be leaving such an enjoyable companion, I wave goodbye and follow Antonio out the door. I silently giggle as I wonder if I had just waved goodbye to a hologram.

---

* * *

Antonio picks up the pace as he wanders into a section of the castle that I'm not familiar with, and I find myself almost jogging to keep up.

"What's wrong, Antonio? Why the urgency? Did something happen to Angela?"

Antonio doesn't respond, just quickly ushers me into a room at the end of the hall. I walk in expecting to see Angela, and am taken aback by the sight before me. I feel like I've just re-entered Russ's dungeon, only with brand new toys! I look back at Antonio for an explanation, just in time to witness him locking us in, then turn to face me with an evil grin. Oh, no. Too late I realize my mistake.

"Lucas, what are you doing?"

Leaning against the door lazily, he takes his time assessing me, giving my body the full once-over.

"We have some unfinished business, baby. It wasn't very nice the way you just up and disappeared on me last time."

"Sorry, it wasn't intentional. I had the timer preset for an hour. The hour was up. Just think how mad you'd be if it had turned off five minutes earlier."

Lucas glares at me and then asks, "So what's the timer set for this time?"

"I . . . uh . . ." Oh my God. I *forgot* to set the timer!

Lucas watches as the panicked expression crosses my face, and then my eyes desperately scan the walls for a life-saving pull station. Not immediately locating one, I turn to Lucas for reassurance.

"Where's the pull station, Lucas?"

"You didn't set the timer this time, did you? And I can assume from your alarmed expression, that hubby is not nearby to rescue you. Oh the fates are smiling upon me right now."

"You can't do this to me, Lucas. It's not safe. You have to let me out of here."

"All in good time, Miranda. All in good time. Let's have a little fun, first."

After a fifteen minute struggle where I invariably emerge the loser, I find myself stark naked with my arms yanked painfully above my head and fastened to the ceiling. For now, I remain standing flat on the floor with my back pressed into a smooth, wooden post. Sweating and panting from exertion, Lucas holds up a one by four wooden plank with metal tabs protruding from one end, and asks me to stand on my tip toes. Knowing that to disobey him in my current situation will only result in pain, I comply.

Lucas spreads my legs so that I'm straddling the wooden plank, narrow sides facing up and down, and inserts the metal tabs into pre-made notches cut into the wooden post behind me. Satisfied, he backs away and gives me permission to relax, no longer being required to remain on my tip toes. As soon as I lower myself, I catch my breath as the hard edges of the wooden plank separate my nether lips and press uncomfortably into my pussy. Lucas just smiles.

---

*　　*　　*

"Ever ridden a wooden horse, Miranda? I can't wait to watch you giddy on up."

"Lucas, you're mad. What did I ever do to you to inspire such contempt?"

"Hmmm, that would be confusing to you, wouldn't it? This should clear things up some."

Lucas turns around and faces the wall, when suddenly my vision begins to blur and waver. But no, everything else is remaining in focus but Lucas. He is blurring. My crotch starts to burn from the constant pressure of the inflexible wooden plank, knowing that I'll soon have to raise up on tiptoes again to help alleviate the pain. I look down as best I can in my current trussed up state to see if it's possible to wriggle free, but discover there is no escaping. I'm stuck here until Lucas decides otherwise. I look up to try and reason with him and scream in terror at the vision before me. No longer am I gazing at Lucas, but another, more frightening apparition. Wit. Oh my God. Lucas is really Wit.

Immediately, I am catapulted back in time and to memories I'd thought long dead and buried. Wit. Back to the first time we had spoken in the chat rooms. Wit. Back to his irresistible opening line, "I know what a woman wants. I know what a woman needs." Wit. Back to that fateful day when I relinquished control and allowed him to call, an encounter that both sickened and thrilled me. Wit. Back to the Vegas elevator, and how he overpowered and took me captive, to be used solely as a plaything, not only for his amusement, but his lovely companion, Rachel's, as well. Wit. Back to how I escaped, physically and emotionally. Wit. Back to all of those conflicting feelings . . . terror . . . acceptance . . . intrigue . . . resistance . . . excitement . . . unrest . . . acquiescence . . . stubbornness . . . enlightenment . . . mystification . . . freedom . . . confinement . . . awareness . . . degradation . . . strength . . . weakness . . . but above all, fright.

I fear his power and control over me. I fear what I'm capable of at his hands. I fear what I become when in his presence. Oh God. And now I find myself right back in his clutches.

"Why?" I croak out. "Why can't you just leave me alone?"

Wit approaches me carrying a latex hood, complete with eyes and nose areas cut open, and a double-ended penis protruding from the mouth portion. Lewdly stroking the outer phallus, Wit explains, "Nobody bests me, Miranda. And nobody disappears from me . . . for very long, that is. You and I have so much more to experience."

"But, Antonio? How?"

"Oh, Antonio really is my brother, just not my twin. That's one of the beauties of VR. You can program the computer to portray your image however you'd like. Antonio has no idea what he's helped me to accomplish. Originally, I used him to search for you, but he found Angela instead. Ultimately, that led me back to you."

Frozen, I can only gape as he inserts the smaller end of the dildo into my mouth, then covers my head with the rest of the hood, zipping it tightly closed in back. Unable to resist, he runs his tongue along the tip of the large appendage protruding from my mouth, mocking me. Suddenly, the horror of the wooden horse has lessened, being eclipsed by the menacing figure standing before me.

"Who would you like to fuck with your face first, Miranda? Raven? Perhaps you'd even like to take *me* for a ride? Wouldn't you like to stick those eight inches right up my ass?"

The last sound I can remember hearing before I pass out and blissfully succumb to the darkness, is his endless evil laughter, "Ha, Ha, Ha, Ha, Ha, Ha, Ha!!!!!!"

CHAPTER 10

■

VALIDATIONS

"Honey, you can't end it with her trapped in VR! The readers will go nuts!"

"You think? They all know that Miranda has a guardian angel following her around. No real harm ever comes to her, just difficult situations."

"Ok, wife, but if you ask me, that's just plain mean."

"Oh really? Has my husband developed a soft spot for her?"

"Uh . . . well . . . maybe."

"Don't worry, darling. I'm sure Nick breaks down the door and rescues her from Wit's clutches in plenty of time."

"Well, as long as you're sure," he says with a wink. "Oh by the way, a letter came for you today."

"Really, from who?"

"Doesn't say. Open it and let's see."

The blood drains from my face as I read the letter:

Someday I will come for you, and you shall experience each and every page of your novels.

ME

Order These Selected Blue Moon Titles

Souvenirs From a Boarding School $7.95
The Captive $7.95
Ironwood Revisited $7.95
Sundancer $7.95
Julia $7.95
The Captive II $7.95
Shadow Lane $7.95
Belle Sauvage $7.95
Shadow Lane III $7.95
My Secret Life $9.95
Our Scene $7.95
Chrysanthemum, Rose & the Samurai $7.95
Captive V $7.95
Bombay Bound $7.95
Sadopaideia $7.95
The New Story of O $7.95
Shadow Lane IV $7.95
Beauty in the Birch $7.95
Laura $7.95
The Reckoning $7.95
Ironwood Continued $7.95
In a Mist $7.95
The Prussian Girls $7.95
Blue Velvet $7.95
Shadow Lane V $7.95
Deep South $7.95

Shades of Singapore $7.95
Images of Ironwood $7.95
What Love $7.95
Sabine $7.95
An English Education $7.95
The Encounter $7.95
Tutor's Bride $7.95
A Brief Education $7.95
Love Lessons $7.95
Shogun's Agent $7.95
The Sign of the Scorpion $7.95
Women of Gion $7.95
Mariska I $7.95
Secret Talents $7.95
Beatrice $7.95
S&M: The Last Taboo $8.95
"Frank" & I $7.95
Lament $7.95
The Boudoir $7.95
The Bitch Witch $7.95
Story of O $5.95
Romance of Lust $9.95
Ironwood $7.95
Virtue's Rewards $5.95
The Correct Sadist $7.95
The New Olympia Reader $15.95

Visit our website at www.bluemoonbooks.com

ORDER FORM
Attach a separate sheet for additional titles.

Title	Quantity	Price
_____	___	_____
_____	___	_____
_____	___	_____
_____	___	_____

Shipping and Handling (see charges below) _____

Sales tax (in CA and NY) _____

Total _____

Name _____

Address _____

City _____ State _____ Zip _____

Daytime telephone number _____

❑ Check   ❑ Money Order   (US dollars only. No COD orders accepted.)

Credit Card # _____ Exp. Date _____

❑ MC   ❑ VISA   ❑ AMEX

Signature _____

(if paying with a credit card you must sign this form.)

Shipping and Handling charges:*

Domestic: $4 for 1st book, $.75 each additional book. International: $5 for 1st book, $1 each additional book
*rates in effect at time of publication. Subject to Change.

Mail order to Publishers Group West, Attention: Order Dept., 1700 Fourth St., Berkeley, CA 94710, or fax to (510) 528-3444.

PLEASE ALLOW 4-6 WEEKS FOR DELIVERY. ALL ORDERS SHIP VIA 4TH CLASS MAIL.

Look for Blue Moon Books at your favorite local bookseller or from your favorite online bookseller.